The BEST Teacher "STUFF"

from Nancy L. Johnson

Pieces of Learning
Division of Creative Learning Consultants

© 1993

Pieces of Learning

ISBN   1-880505-06-1

Printing 10987654

Table of "STUFF"

Acknowledgements

Joe Wayman
for the thousands of hours spent together planning, brainstorming, arguing, and presenting workshops together.

Glenn Poshard
for fighting the good fight for Illinois education and who now continues the fight as Congressman Poshard.
I knew you when....Glendal!

Kathy, Stan, and Pat
for using their organizing, editing, and layout skills on all this STUFF!

To all the important people who have shared great ideas.

Life on the Road

"On the road again; I just can't wait to get on the road again." I wonder Willie! How many weather-delayed flights, lost suitcases, airport mystery meat hot dogs, and no-tell motels are there in a consultant's life?

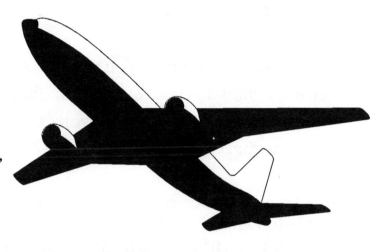

Teachers comment, *"I'd love to do what you do! It must be so wonderful and glamorous traveling all over the country!"* My father, a retired farmer, has his own special way of putting my life in perspective. He loves to tell the neighbors how ***Creative Learning Consultants*** spreads me all over the country just like manure!

Actually, the good outweighs the bad. There are wonderful, fascinating, and sometimes surprising people in my 17 years of travel. In Nova Scotia I experienced some of the most beautiful scenery and nicest people—including Jill, the Canadian customs agent who looked bewildered as I explained how pieces of yarn, masking tape, feathers, colored dots, and puzzle pieces enlighten Canadian educators!

Not all experiences include humans. In Montana a rattlesnake crawling in the hall of my motel surprised me! Not much stands in the way of my addiction to Diet Pepsi! The snake (Rocky) was between me and the thirst-quenching machine. I decided I could turn that critter around and herd it out the door. Rocky would have none of that! He coiled right up and with help from his rattles proclaimed ownership of the hall. Plan B consisted of one respectful, not quite as brave, education consultant backing into her room and reaching for the telephone. I wonder if the bath towel I rolled up and jammed under my door that night is still there . . .

"stuff"

stuff (stuf),n. 1.a good fundamental material of which anything is made. 2.things, belongings, fabric. 3.*an artistic product of unspecified kind*. 4.*Informal, a special skill:*to do one's stuff. 5. *v.* to fill up. 6.to fill or cram into an opening. 7.to pack tightly. 8.**TO DO GOOD STUFF—THE ONLY STUFF!**

"Hey! I remember you. You're that "Feather Lady."

"Are we going to tie each other up with yarn again?"

"I still have my red dot from your last workshop."

"Guess what? My airplane partner sent me a birthday card!"

It's true. The memory experts are right. People remember "stuff" they DO better than "stuff" they HEAR. It's always fun when teachers stop me at conferences to remind me of a workshop I did at their school. It's the learning by doing activities that stick in the memory bank. Joyce Ritchie, I will never forget you. When you opened your checkbook that day at the Ohio Career Education Conference and pulled out a bright pink feather that had been taped to the inside cover, my heart skipped a beat. And then, when you told me you had been carrying it since 1985, you took my breath away! Thank you, dear friend. It's people like you that make a difference.

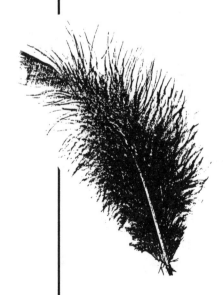

Teachers are forever looking for more teaching "stuff." They never seem to have enough. Of course, their need for "stuff" changes as new bandwagons roll through education. However, some of the best "stuff" is the old "stuff"—those tried and true strategies that seem to work year after year. Either way, new "stuff"/old "stuff," when students are physically, intellectually, and emotionally involved in learning it's the BEST "STUFF." The learn-by-doing activities in this book are the most popular, most asked for, most complimented, and most remembered of all those I have shared during workshops. Enjoy!
It's GOOD "STUFF!"

Goals for Students

. . . to use my imagination

. . . to have fun learning

. . . to express my own feelings and views

. . . to learn how to think harder and better

. . . to learn to work independently

. . . to learn to work with others

. . . to think in different ways

. . . to think of new ways to
    do things

. . . to discipline my mind

. . . to share my ideas with
    others

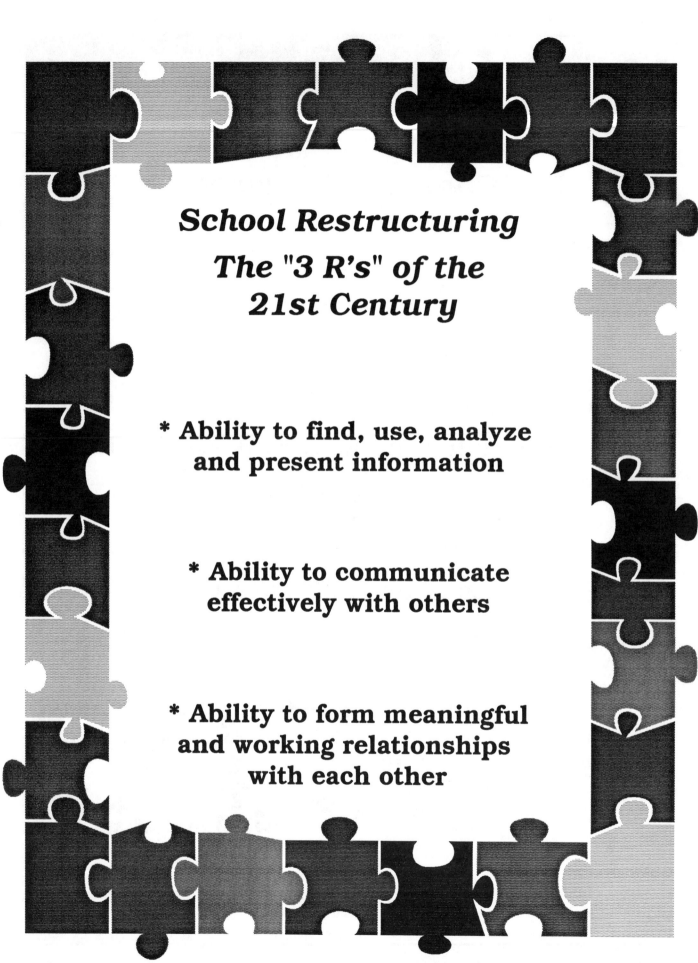

School Restructuring
The "3 R's" of the 21st Century

* Ability to find, use, analyze and present information

* Ability to communicate effectively with others

* Ability to form meaningful and working relationships with each other

8

Even if you're on the right track,

You'll get run over if you just sit there.

—Will Rogers

The federal government can show leadership,

but the only way we're going to improve our schools—

and therefore our country—

is one student at a time

and one school at a time.

—John Akers, CEO, IBM

For All Those Born Before 1945

We are Survivors!

Consider the changes we have witnessed:

We were born **before** television, penicillin, polio shots, frozen foods, xerox, plastic, contact lenses, frisbees, and "the pill."

We were born **before** radar, credit cards, split atoms, laser beams and ballpoint pens, **before** panty-hose, dishwashers, clothes dryers, electric blankets, air conditioners, drip-dry clothes—and **before** man walked on the moon.

—*Joe Wayman*

We got married **FIRST** and then lived together. How quaint can you be?

In our time, **closets** were for clothes, not for "coming out of." **Rabbits** were not Volkswagens, and **having a meaningful relationship** meant getting along well with our cousins.

We thought **fast food** was what you ate during Lent, and **outer space** was the back of the Riviera Theater.

We were born **before** house-husbands, gay rights, computer dating, dual careers and computer marriages. We were born **before** day-care centers, group therapy and nursing homes. We never heard of FM radio, tape decks, electric typewriters, artificial hearts, word processors, yogurt, and guys wearing earrings. For us, **time-sharing** meant togetherness—not computers or condominiums: a **chip** meant a piece of wood; **hardware** meant hardware, and **software** wasn't even a word!

In 1940, **Made in Japan** meant junk and the term **making out** referred to how you did on your exam. Pizzas, McDonald's and instant coffee were unheard of.

We hit the scene when there were 5 cent and 10 cent stores where you bought things for five and ten cents. For one nickel you could ride a street car (trolley), make a phone call, buy a Pepsi or enough stamps to mail one letter and two postcards. You could buy a new Chevy Coupe for $600, but who could afford one; a pity, too, because gas was 11 cents a gallon!

In our day, cigarette smoking was fashionable, grass was mowed, coke was a drink and pot was something you cooked in. Rock music was a Grandma's lullaby and AIDS were helpers in the principal's office.

We were certainly not born before the difference between the sexes was discovered, but we were surely born before the sex change. We made do with what we had, and we were the last generation that was so dumb as to think you needed a husband to have a baby.

No wonder we are so confused and there is such a generation gap today!

But we survived! What better reason to celebrate!

—*author unknown*
Source: Ohio Career Education Program

—*Joe Wayman*

One Day in the Life of an American Child

17,051 women get pregnant.

2,795 of them are teenagers.

1,106 teenagers have abortions.

372 teenagers miscarry.

1,295 teenagers give birth.

689 babies are born to women who have had inadequate prenatal care.

67 babies die before one month of life.

105 babies die before their first birthday.

719 babies are born at low birth weight (less than 5 pounds, 8 oz)

27 children die from poverty.

10 children die from guns.

30 children are wounded by guns.

6 teenagers commit suicide.

135,000 children bring a gun to school.

7,742 teens become sexually active.

623 teenagers get syphilis or gonorrhea.

211 children are arrested for drug abuse.

437 children are arrested for drinking or drunken driving.

1,512 teenagers drop out of school.

1,849 children are abused or neglected.

3,288 children run away from home.

1,629 children are in adult jails.

2,989 see their parents divorced.

34,285 people lose jobs.

—Harvey Alston, educational consultant, Best, Inc. Columbus OH

20 Top Jobs for the Year 2000

Occupation	Projected salary in the year 2000

Biggest percentage increase

Occupation	Salary
Paralegal professionals	$45,400
Medical assistants	$20,000-$32,000
Physical therapists	$53,000
Physical and corrective therapy assistants and aides	$30,000-$36,000
Data processing equipment repairers	$54,000
Home health aides	$20,000
Podiatrists	$127,000
Computer systems analysts and electronic data processing professionals	$66,000
Medical record technicians	$33,000
Employment interviewers and employment service professionals	$32,000-$48,000

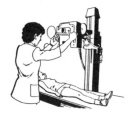

✗ Top states for jobs—greatest percentage growth by the year 2000

New Hampshire	Nevada
Arizona	New Jersey
Florida	Colorado
Alaska	California
Utah	New Mexico

Most new jobs

retail salespeople $23,000

waiters and waitresses $18,000

registered nurses $48,000

janitors, cleaners, maids, and housekeepers

                                                                        $26,000

general managers and top executives $69,000

cashiers $19,000

truck drivers $46,000

general office clerks $30,000

food counter and fountain workers $16,000

nursing aides, orderlies, and attendants $22,000

✓ Greatest NUMBER of new jobs

California	Illinois
Texas	Ohio
New York	New Jersey
Florida	Michigan
Pennsylvania	North Carolina

Perhaps learning should be a
life-long journey,
not a 13-year race.

On the Road Again

Hurry Up And Wait !

Life has furnished me with many teachers: Mom, Dad, Grandma Onie, Miss Peterson, Mrs. Kenward, Bobby D., Buckminster Fuller, Brian, Tom, Rosie, Jose, John Warren, Kathy, Stan, Joey, Stevie, Sam I Am (the super cat), my dog Brownie, a cow named Bessie, and various other acquaintances including a few total strangers.

The latest addition to my list of teachers lacks two or even four legs. This inhuman lesson giver happens to be a long gray slab of concrete covered in asphalt, tar, grease, dirt, white lines, and 9 million cars. An arrogant expressway that winds through a seemingly never ending chain of suburbs that cling to the city of Chicago. This six lane engineering marvel collects 40 cents every six miles from all unsuspecting drivers foolish enough to accept its challenge. Yes, it's the 294 Tri-State Tollway. And as the kids would say, "*IT'S AWESOME!*"

The first hint of trouble came with the cars speeding toward me in the on-coming lane, all moving four times as fast as those of us plodding along in the opposite direction. Even so, I remained preoccupied with what was waiting for me at the end of my journey, a much needed week of "catch up" in the office. Eyes on the end, ignoring the now. Just hurry up and get there. As I slowly passed an exit ramp I saw a hitchhiker thumbing his way to Florida. Of course nobody stopped. We were all in too big of a hurry, rushing at breakneck speed (25 miles per hour) to reach our destinations.

The radio provided the second warning of potential doom. An eighteen wheeler had jack-knifed some 15 miles ahead, oozing its dangerous cargo. That explained the three police cruisers, four fire trucks, two ambulances, two fire chief station wagons, and one hazardous material van that passed me on the right.

Then it happened. Gridlock. Bumper to bumper, all three lanes came to a full stop. Couldn't go forward, couldn't back up, couldn't turn around. No escape! Trapped! The truckers call it PARKING LOT!

As if some great lesson plan book had been opened on the hood of my car, I became a captive yet reluctant student. The course title: PATIENCE 294. There were a couple of pop quizzes that had to be passed before the final exam. The first was DENIAL. Some hyperactive fellow students got out of their cars craning their necks looking for an exit. A couple of slow learners honked their horns as if the aggravating noise would loosen the giant knot of cars. The guy who tried to turn around and ended up wedged between a semi and the guard rail must have been an escapee from an L D class.

It wasn't long before most of us moved on to the second quiz, ACCEPTANCE. Reading, listening to the radio, and sleeping seemed to be the most popular answers. One gifted student started flirting with a woman sitting in a shiny Jag two lanes over, sailing paper airplanes at her windshield. All the "left brainers" were frantically talking on their cellular phones and writing copious notes. Me?—I calmly read the newspaper. Then I read it again. And again. ***And again.*** (If any of you readers ever need to know what happened in the world on August 31, 1992, just ask yours truly. If it was written up in *USA TODAY*, I'll probably be able to quote it line by line!)

I was beginning to feel proud of myself—so calm, collected, and patient; ready to give myself an "*A*". Then I started watching the cars speeding by in the opposite direction. I could feel my blood pressure inching up. I was jealous. I was mad. I hated them all. How dare they grin and wave? Surely they must all be exceeding the speed limit just for spite. I started dreaming about a SWAT team descending down on them and arresting them ALL! So much for calm and collected. So much for my "*A*".

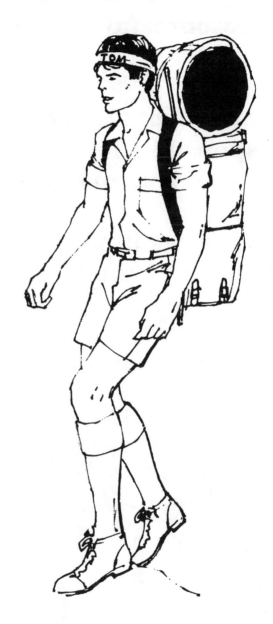

And then came the final blow, the straw that broke the camel's back, the final exam, the ultimate test of human endurance and patience: the hitch-hiker came **WALKING** by, getting closer and closer to Florida.

I wonder who waits in our classrooms . . .

If we want children to learn to think and read, we must show them thoughtful people eager to take in new information.

If we want them to be brave and resourceful, let them see us risking a new idea or finding a way.

If we want them to be loyal, patriotic and responsible, let us show them that we can be true to our deepest principles.

If we want new and better schools, we will have to be new and better people...

And wasn't that what we always wanted?

—Marilyn Ferguson, *Towards a Quantum Mind, Vancouver, BC, May 1986*

20

On The Road . . . Again

Rod Serling's haunting words, "You have just entered the Twilight Zone," echoed silently around me as I walked out of the school. I stopped and looked back to remind myself that it was reality, not some nightmarish fantasy, that was making my heart pound. My mind was spinning as I felt a confusion of anger, surprise, and love.

My sudden surge of high blood pressure was caused by a row of Abraham Lincoln profiles, neatly taped along a brick hallway in a school I had been visiting. Each one had been outlined and colored exactly the same—except one. There were 24 identical black beards and ties—except one. Twenty-four Abes, each adorned in the upper left corner with a large, carefully printed, red letter "*A*"—except one.

Bradley's profile of Abe was the exception. He had colored the tie a beautiful bright red. And there for all to see was Bradley's embarrassment—in the upper left corner, a large, carefully printed, red letter "*F*".

The line of Abes on the wall ended at the door of a first grade classroom. There I had shifted my gaze to the red tie, to the "*F*", to the door, and back to the tie again, wondering about the motives of the teacher who had given the "*F*" and about Bradley, who had received it.

I knocked on the door. To this day, I don't remember the teacher, what she looked like, or how she reacted when I asked to speak to Bradley. But I will never forget Bradley. When he saw me, he smiled and said, "You're that funny lady we listened to in the gym this morning!" As we looked at his picture, I told him I really liked it. I took a blue marker from my purse, rubbed out the red "*F*", and replaced it with a large, carefully printed, blue "*A*". I asked Bradley if I could have his Abraham Lincoln to display on my refrigerator at home. He smiled shyly and nodded yes.

The tension binding the teacher, Bradley, and me was suddenly shattered by the recess bell. Bradley reached for his coat, the teacher walked into her classroom, and I headed out into the new year 1993.

As I walked toward my car, Bradley waved to me from the playground. "Bradley!" I shouted, "*I think Abe Lincoln would have LOVED that red tie!*"

If you think you can

or think you can't—

You're
ABSOLUTELY Right!

—Henry Ford

On The Road . . . Again

He might have been a fisherman; the red and white Igloo cooler hiding his catch, frozen just long enough to survive one plane trip and a fast car ride to a waiting freezer. Then again he might have been a college student heading back to the dorm with some well-preserved home cooking that would soon be competing with the mystery food in the cafeteria. The torn blue jeans, faded sweatshirt, and old sneakers were fairly obvious clues or so I assumed.

We traveling people watchers take great pride in correctly guessing what our subjects do for a living, where they are going, and why. All just by looking, of course. It's all based on ASSUMPTIONS. A few of us have been known to come right out and ask perfect strangers about the truth of our assumptions. We can't stand the suspense! Some would say we are curious, others nosey.

It seems to me, we humans assume so much from so little. We are so quick to pass judgments based on assumptions. The way someone looks, a slight turn of the body, an unusual voice pattern, and we just KNOW he or she . . . etc., etc.

The assumptions we adults make about each other are usually harmless. However, we educators sometimes make assumptions about students that could make or break a fragile self-concept.

"Mary will never do any better in school because her older sister wasn't a good student."

"It is so obvious. Greg is destined to be a great basketball player because he is so tall."

"Tina has such fine manners because she comes from a 'good' family."

"It's no wonder Katie got pregnant at age fifteen. She always wore such suggestive clothes."

"Matt played with dolls in pre-school and hated sports. He must be gay."

"Mrs. Brown is a welfare mother. That is why her children are unmotivated."

"Oh, my gosh! I just found out I have the low class. It's going to be a long year!"

We give ourselves away, you know. Our students pick it up like sonar. Our behavior creates behavior. We can choose to make negative or positive assumptions. The responsibility for such a choice is, as the kids say, AWESOME!

By the way, remember the guy with the cooler? We sat together on a flight to Minneapolis. The plane that had been chartered for him had a mechanical problem so he was hitching a ride on a commercial jet. He was a surgeon, on his way to assist in a transplant operation. The Igloo had a human heart in it.

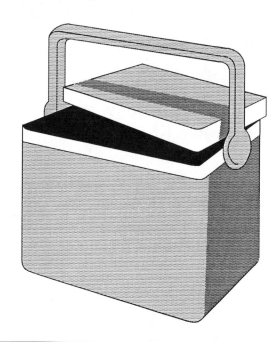

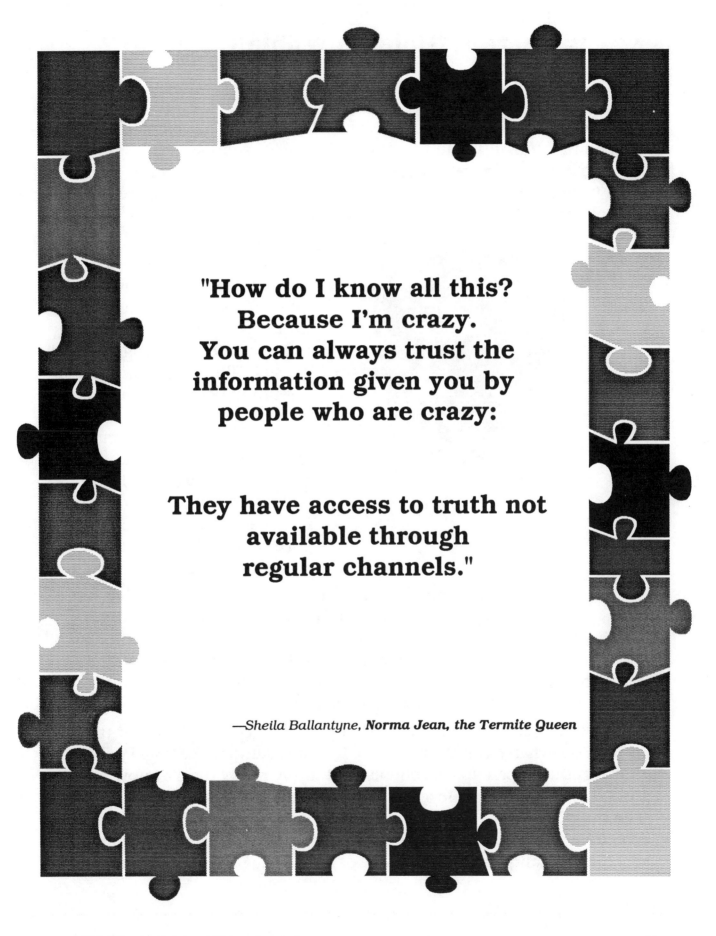

"How do I know all this?
Because I'm crazy.
You can always trust the
information given you by
people who are crazy:

They have access to truth not
available through
regular channels."

—Sheila Ballantyne, **Norma Jean, the Termite Queen**

Is There A "Hole" in Whole Language?

Perhaps it's because of what I do for a living, traveling around the country consulting in literally hundreds of schools. Perhaps it's my age, having survived in education for 25 years. More than likely it's a feeling—an uncomfortable feeling—that too many children in school are **TEACHING THEMSELVES**.

The problem is like a two-headed dragon with one head labeled *Cooperative Learning* and the other *Whole Language*. I really don't want to appear to be a dragon slayer. Killing such an interesting unique creature would be a mistake. Some positive and useful changes have occurred since *Whole Language* and *Cooperative Learning* hit the education scene. For the past few years they have been the core of what is new and innovative in elementary schools.

However, "new" is always difficult in education. As so often happens, many school districts jump on the latest bandwagon without monitoring its progress or considering the consequences. And once they are on the wagon (after spending a lot of time and money) they are afraid to stop or even slow down long enough to ask: "Is this REALLY working the way it's supposed to?"

I can't help but be reminded of the *Open School Concept* that hit in the 70's when I was a first grade teacher. Almost overnight school districts built open space schools, but many really didn't know how to utilize them to their fullest extent let alone get back their investment. The buildings looked great from the outside, but inside it was a different story. Many teachers weren't prepared for the extensive changes in teaching techniques that the concept required. Slowly but surely screens, portable shelves, temporary dividers, and finally permanent walls appeared.

The *Whole Language* bandwagon has rolled through many school districts. There is no doubt it has brought with it many innovative ideas and approaches to teaching reading. Many teachers have been pulled away from their "reading bible"—namely basal readers. They have been given more freedom to use their professional judgement in making decisions about children and literacy, especially in the area of evaluation.

Thanks to *Whole Language* many children are allowed to explore beautiful trade books as they learn to read, which in turn has drawn library/ media specialists into the "learning to read trenches" where they belong. It has also empowered children to learn various skills when THEY want to learn them rather than when the teacher dictates. Some would say *Whole Language* is a "child centered" approach to reading while the basal reader is a "teacher centered" approach. Most important, the *Whole Language* philosophy views children as communicators who are writers as well as readers. Sounds great. So what's the problem? Where is the "hole?"

The *Whole Language* philosophy encourages teachers to seize on "teachable moments" to present important skills. Teachers must be prepared and confident enough to "fly by the seat of their pants" and rely on unplanned instruction. But what if these so called "teachable moments" don't occur? When are the missed skills taught? And by whom? What if a new, inexperienced or weak teacher doesn't recognize the "teachable moments?"

How many school districts have enough money to offer the extra training and inservice required to bring such teachers up to speed? And the most painful question of all: Does education really have enough teacher talent to meet the challenges of *Whole Language*? Does the entire concept ask too much in time and energy from today's busy classroom teachers, many of whom are full time wives, mothers, and career women?

—*Joe Wayman*

The dragon breathes even more fire. Part of the *Whole Language* philosophy dictates that even though teachers may take advantage of "teachable moments" to introduce new skills, students are not necessarily required to MASTER them. Teachers need only to MENTION the skills.

The real danger is that students may learn only enough to be able to complete the current lesson but not enough to really apply the skill in other situations. Another part of that philosophy maintains that children will NATURALLY DISCOVER many of the skills they will need to become good readers. They will make the right decisions about which strategy is best for them to use in learning to read. But, are ALL children really capable of making such decisions?

More than one expert has offered evidence that not all children naturally discover reading skills on their own. (Adams, 1990) Some slow learners, learning disabled, and minority students will not "find their own way into literacy." (Delpit, 1991) Many children from disadvantaged language backgrounds are unable to "discover" WHAT they need, WHEN they need it, and HOW they should learn it. As a result, they make many more errors on reading achievement tests. (Rosenshine, 1984)

Some *Whole Language* proponents would say that standardized reading tests are out of date, ineffective, and should not be used. That may be. But that is not the real world. Standardized tests are still widely used. As long as we have such tests, administrators, school boards, and teachers should bear the responsibility to teach children what they need to know in order to make a decent score.

First throw out the tests—then come talk to me about how they are not important!

Children from middle or upper class neighborhoods show up at school already knowing many of the language rules and codes that make learning to read much easier. This gives them a tremendous power to play the traditional American "school game." However, many minority children, especially those growing up in poverty, have not been saturated with the same cultural experiences. The culture they come from is not necessarily bad, wrong, or inferior—just different. They are, in effect, not playing on a level field with other children.

A good teacher can make that playing field level by teaching the skills these children need along with an understanding of WHY they need them. Delpit (1988) quotes one African American mother: "My kids know how to be Black—you all teach them how to be successful in the White man's world." What the African American mother is talking about is POWER. It takes a good teacher using DIRECT SYSTEMATIC INSTRUCTION to empower minority children with the REAL skills they need to be successful in the REAL world.

IN DEFENSE OF DIRECT SYSTEMATIC INSTRUCTION:

"An extensive body of research indicates that clearly defined objectives and teacher directed instruction are characteristics of effective reading programs. This research shows that learning is more likely to occur if students know what the learning tasks are and if teachers specifically teach them. Sustained direct instruction has as one of its goals that learners will indeed learn from the lesson and the job is not considered completed until transfer has occurred, that is, until the students can use the strategy with new, authentic materials for authentic purposes."

—Dr. Dixie Lee Spiegel

Direct instruction can be as innovative, creative, and exciting as *Whole Language*, "Half Language", or any other approach to literacy. As always, **THE TEACHER MAKES THE DIFFERENCE**, not the program. However, Direct Systematic Instruction should NOT give teachers permission to stand at the front of the class and lecture, lecture, lecture! "Skilling and drilling" is mindless teaching under any label.

At its best, Direct Systematic Instruction involves a powerful one-two-three punch that teaches children to read.

1. The teacher/facilitator describes to students situations when a specific reading skill might be needed. (Why is reading important and when is it needed? What are our goals and objectives?)

2. The teacher/facilitator models how to select the correct strategy from several alternatives. (What are all the different ways that we can learn a reading skill? Which one can the teacher model? Which one might work best for the student?)

3. Students master the skills through creative guided and independent application monitored by the teacher. (Which student knows which skill? Are pre/posts appropriate? Does instruction need to be changed? What many and varied ways can we use what we have learned?)

Students need strong, confident, teachers to observe them, work with them, and make good choices about a curriculum that provides experiences that fit their needs. Reading is not a natural process like spoken language. For many children reading is a tough, complicated, even mysterious process that deserves adult guidance. Too many children grow weary of "discovering" how to read. They need to be taught.

At its best, reading instruction involves the **COMBINATION** of many approaches. Any good teacher, worth his or her salt, knows there is no such thing as **THE** method. What works for one child will not work for another. What worked last year will not work this year. What works in one school district will be a complete failure in another. Colleges and universities should train future teachers how to pull from several methods and strategies. An inflexible either/or approach to how to teach will certainly lead to failure. Those *Whole Language* proponents who demand that school districts **ADOPT** their philosophy rather than **ADAPT** it are doing children a great disservice.

THE BEST OF TWO WORLDS

The very best professional dancers continue to take dance class throughout their careers. They need the constant guidance of a master teacher. They also rely on choreographers to provide quality material for them to interpret. This creative mix of choreography, individual talent and style result in a beautiful, satisfying experience for teacher and student.

In much the same way, teachers of reading choreograph creative curriculum and provide systematic direct instruction that motivates and guides students as they "dance" through the process of learning to read.

References

Adams, M. (1990) **Beginning To Read: Thinking And Learning About Print.** Cambridge, MA:MIT Press.

Delpit, L.D. (1988). **The Silenced Dialogue: Power And Pedagogy In Educating Other People's Children.** *Harvard Educational Review*, 58, 280-298.

Delpit, L.D. (1991). **A Conversation With Lisa Delpit.** *Language Arts*, 68, 541-547.

Rosenshine, B., & Stevens, R. (1984). **Classroom Instruction In Reading**. In P.D. Pearson (Ed.), *Handbook Of Reading Research* (pp. 745-798). New York: Longman.

Spiegel, Dixie Lee. (1992). **Blending Whole Language and Systematic Direct Instruction.** *The Reading Teacher*, Vol. 46, No. 1, September.

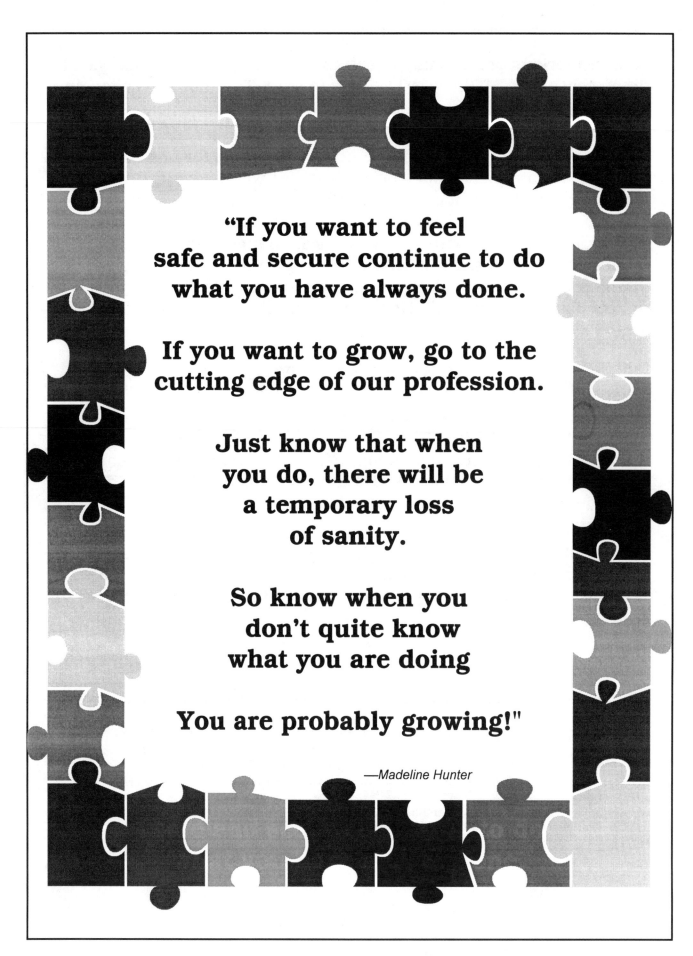

"If you want to feel
safe and secure continue to do
what you have always done.

If you want to grow, go to the
cutting edge of our profession.

Just know that when
you do, there will be
a temporary loss
of sanity.

So know when you
don't quite know
what you are doing

You are probably growing!"

—*Madeline Hunter*

"Children

are the living messages

we send to a time

we will not see."

—author unknown

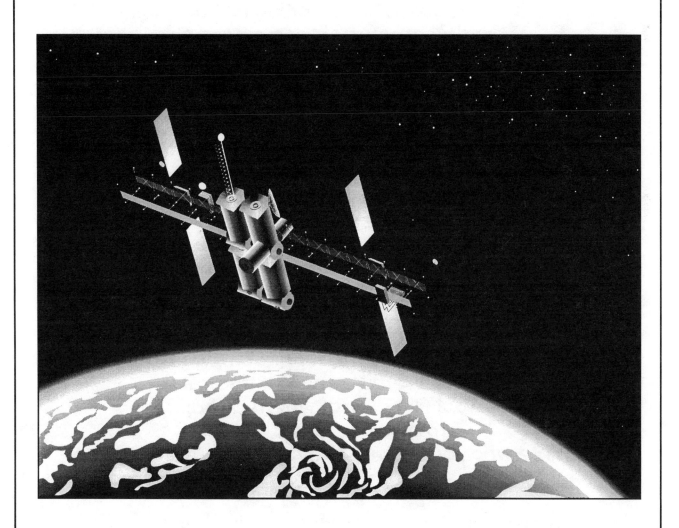

To My Kids

You know I can't understand you today
You're such idiots
Why don't you understand that I trust you
That I really care for you
Why do you insist on betraying my trust
Don't you know by now
That I am not a policeman
I am a person, a human being just like you,
and when you betray me it hurts.
Do you know that the really important thing
to me is not that you learn about
Caesar's Rome or Washington's leadership
But that you learn about you.
Why, when I leave you, must you act as
Small children, quibbling over petty things,
Telling dirty jokes, throwing things.
When will you learn that the true test
Of Being a Real Person, a Mature Being
Is how you carry yourself when you are alone,
Away from me and anyone else who represents authority.
It is easy to be the kind of people you are today.
It doesn't require any self control
To heave a paper wad across the room when I'm gone.
It doesn't require any self-discipline
To spill out filthy words when you happen
to be alone as a class.
OK! OK! Be who you are or whoever it is you're trying to be
But you will not make a failure out of me
Because, after all
I've made up my mind to love you more this spring
Than I did last fall.

by Glenn Poshard

The Long Haired Kids With Guitars

Hey by God! I just heard your music
on electric guitars for the first time
And I'm over forty
I wasn't listening before.

I thought it was noisy
And forgot that twenty year olds
Feel love, and God, and pain
And have formulated some philosophy.

What was the matter with me?
You just changed the scenery
Christ is in Rock 'n Roll
And your preachin' is in night clubs.

You know something!
There's a lot of good poetry around,
Two for a quarter on the juke box
And we haven't been paying attention.

Hey Friends! Excuse me for not listenin'
You saw what older eyes forgot about.
I'm going to get change for a dollar
and remind myself to feel again.

By Bob Davis

*(Bobby D. was a friend and mentor who always told the truth about education
and life. He lived what he believed, without excuses. And he never stopped learning.)*

Fences

I wasn't good at kickball.
As a catcher I was bad.
The basketball eluded me.
As a runner it was sad.

But one thing I was good at,
Better than the rest.
When it came to climbing fences,
Clearly, I was best.

I'd hit a fence at sixty,
Grabbing madly for the top,
Throw one leg over, then the next,
Push away and drop!

Landing on the other side,
With a soft but solid plop,
I'd conquered one more fence,
And for the moment I could stop.

'Cause fences are like mountains,
At least to kids of eight or nine,
Just begging to be conquered,
Just waiting to be climbed.

Now grown-ups say that fences
Let you know where you should be.
Like rules we have to live by,
They keep things orderly.

from
DON'T BURN DOWN THE
BIRTHDAY CAKE

But when I was a kid,
Somehow I didn't know.
So breaking all the rules,
Over fences I would go.

And now that I am all grown up,
It seems to me I find,
Some people building fences
Of a very different kind.

As long as some folks build them,
Build them high or build them wide,
I'll keep on climbing fences,
I need to know the other side.

And for every fence they build,
When all is done and said,
I think I'll try, for all my days,
To build a bridge instead.

Joe Wayman
Dec 6, 1988

Coffee Table Christmas

The most important lessons of life are those taught by the most important teachers—parents. They are usually gentle lessons, taught in the simplest context at the most unexpected times yet resulting in a profound and lasting impression.

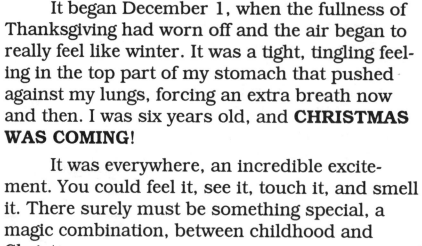

It began December 1, when the fullness of Thanksgiving had worn off and the air began to really feel like winter. It was a tight, tingling feeling in the top part of my stomach that pushed against my lungs, forcing an extra breath now and then. I was six years old, and **CHRISTMAS WAS COMING**!

It was everywhere, an incredible excitement. You could feel it, see it, touch it, and smell it. There surely must be something special, a magic combination, between childhood and Christmas.

Of course, adults were affected too. Mrs. Stevenson, my teacher, was smiling all the time, motivated no doubt by a sudden rash of good behavior exhibited by her students following a class letter to Santa Claus. (Surely Santa would remember all our good deeds and overlook a few minor indescretions.)

The requests for presents covered several pages; my list was among the longest. It seemed like the whole world was turning around me, getting ready to celebrate with me, purchasing gifts for me. Yes, I was reminded in Sunday School that our gifts to one another were really symbols of gifts to the Christ Child. But when you are six years old and you know there will be dolls and games and toys and maybe even a pony on Christmas morning well, it's hard to focus on "the giving" when your mind is bursting with "the getting."

It was an especially cold winter. Our farm had been covered with a thick, glazed blanket of snow for weeks. I remember how the snow cracked and squeaked under my feet in the sub-zero mornings as I walked from the house to the corncrib to do my chores. The corncrib was my favorite place on the farm. It was a place to work and play, a place to dream, and a place to share thoughts and feelings with special friends.

When you are a farm kid, with no brothers or sisters, and you live several miles from town, your special friends are critters so you talk to them. Brownie knew just what I wanted for Christmas. He'd bark and wag his tail when I would describe in great detail, including hand signals and sound effects, all the toys I had asked for. And I knew that Snowball's silky white fur felt just like the hair of that Tony doll I had picked out of the catalog. She'd purr and stretch when I talked about the tea parties the three of us would have. The pattern was set: there would be time to decorate the house, time for church on Christmas Eve, time for a big dinner, and time for me to open my presents!

Then, unexpectedly, the pattern changed. It was three days before Christmas. I looked out my bedroom window because Brownie was barking. Dad had just come home from town and had parked the pickup truck down by the corncrib instead of up by the house. My mom didn't notice because she was in the basement washing clothes.

Dad hollered for me from the porch. "Get your duds on and come out to the crib," he said. "Hurry up!" I didn't know what was going on. But when your dad is 6'6" tall and weighs over 200 pounds and says hurry up you hurry up! I pulled on my snowsuit in record time, tugged at my boots, and ran out the door, fumbling with my mittens and scarf. Brownie had beaten me to the crib by 30 seconds and was sitting patiently at Dad's feet waiting for me.

Dad proceeded to unload a large, strange-looking object from the pickup. Before I had time to ask, he said, "It's a new coffee table for your mom. We can surprise her with it on Christmas morning." My eyes grew wide with excitement as he tore a bit of the protective paper from one corner so I could see it. The wood was a beautiful mahogany, so shiny and smooth that it reflected the light like a mirror.

"What do ya think?" he asked. "Isn't it somethin'? Pretty fancy, huh?" I'm not sure which is more vivid in my memory, the glow of that wood or of Dad's smile! In either case, it was a very special moment. The next few seconds were filled with hugs, squeals of joy, lots of jumping up and down, and a barking dog! When things settled down, we carefully placed the plainly wrapped treasure on a pile of corn in the corner of the crib.

"Now don't let on to your mom what's out here!" Dad said. "It's a surprise, remember?" My eyes met Dad's and we both smiled again. It was the first real secret we had ever shared.

Brownie tilted his head first one way then the other, looking at the strange object that had invaded his territory. He sniffed the paper and licked the string trying to understand why two humans made such a fuss over something that wasn't even fit to eat! I shook my finger at his nose, lectured him about the expense of fine furniture, and threatened him with all sorts of punishments if he even got near it.

The next three days were filled with new emotions as well as several trips to the corncrib just to check on things! I was also experiencing some new and different feelings of anticipation. My excitement about Christmas was stronger than ever, but the tingling sensation pushing against my lungs no longer reminded me of all the presents waiting for me. All I thought about was Mom and that coffee table.

The day before Christmas, I took Snowball with me to the crib. I told her all about the surprise, how the wood felt just as smooth and silky as her fur, and how I could hardly wait to see the look on Mom's face when she saw the coffee table for the first time.

When Christmas morning finlly arrived, I bounded down the stairs to find Mom and Dad eating breakfast at the kitchen table. I headed straight for the porch and my snowsuit and boots. Mom seemed surprised that I was more interested in getting dressed to go outside than I was in opening gifts.

"Don't you want to look under the Christmas tree?" she asked. "I think there are some presents there for you."

As I tugged at my boots, I replied, "Later! Dad and I have to go outside and get something. Come on, Dad. Hurry up! HURRY up!" (When your six-year-old daughter wants to race out into sub-zero weather, skip breakfast, delay opening her Christmas gifts, and insists that you hurry up you hurry up!)

I ran to the crib, beating Brownie by 30 seconds, all the time hollering to Dad to hurry even more. Finally, Dad carried the brown, strangely shaped object to the house and waited with it on the porch while I made Mom sit in the living room with her eyes closed. Then into the living room came the brown object, the father, the kid, the dog, the cat, and lots of dripping snow! SURPRISE! Mom gently unwrapped the table, treating the brown paper as carefully as she would the most expensive tissue. As the shining mahogany began to reveal itself, my mother's face became more beautiful than I had ever remembered it. A glow of surprise mixed with tears and smiles covered her face. There were many feelings spoken but no words. Between the "ooh's" and "ahh's" she first gently stroked the coffee table, then my head, and then my father's face.

For the first time in my young life, I had experienced the pride and pure joy that gift giving can bring. My father had taught me an important lesson that cold December, a lesson about giving and receiving, a lesson that repeated itself every time I saw my mother dust that coffee table. There were other gifts that Christmas morning, but what they were and who received them was lost in the warm glow of mahogany.

MERRY CHRISTMAS, DAD

Guidelines for Developing Units

Design curricular units to develop thinking skills. Emphasize the following teaching strategies:

1. Help the learners to probe a subject *in depth.*

2. Provide an opportunity to utilize *higher-level thought processes* on a regular basis, especially divergent-evaluative thinking.

3. Assist learners in demonstrating *self-motivation* in some discipline.

4. Provide, on a regular basis, multiple opportunities to be *creative.*

5. Provide an educational framework within which students can challenge and stimulate *each other* and share learning experiences designed to help them use their talents productively.

6. Provide multiple opportunities for *self-expression.*

7. Provide opportunities for learners to demonstrate *perseverance* in the face of obstacles.

8. Assist learners to master research skills for *independence and discovery.*

9. Assist learners in assuming *responsibility* for their own learning.

10. Reduce the amount of teacher talk—lectures. Increase student inquiry talking—*interaction.*

11. Insist on *multi resources* in the study of the unit, using books and numerous other types of references.

12. Include *evaluative techniques* as part of the original unit.

13. Encourage "*hidden talent*" to reveal itself during regular class time.

14. Provide *sequential activities* progressing from lower level learning activities to high level activities.

--adapted from LTI consultant Dr. Sandra Kaplan

Learner Outcomes

1. The student will demonstrate the capacity to **apply, analyze, synthesize** and **evaluate** printed materials to accomplish written exercises.

2. The student will demonstrate an ability to undertake library research in order to **gather data** for the completion of assignments.

3. The student will **exhibit fluency** in producing ideas by citing multiple responses in those activities calling for large numbers of responses.

4. The student will evidence an ability to **interact easily** with others by readily participating in the planned group activities.

5. The student will demonstrate an ability to **use social skills** in participating in group activities.

6. The student will demonstrate an ability to **articulate ideas** clearly during the group activities.

7. The student will demonstrate the ability to **use acceptable grammar and punctuation** in writing.

8. The student will **demonstrate organizational ability** through the completion of an acceptable written composition.

9. The student will show an ability to **recognize** the skills and abilities of others by **sharing** products and abilities and reinforcing the efforts of peers.

10. The student will **depict visually** two remote or commonly disassociated ideas.

11. The student will demonstrate an ability to **redefine elements of a task** by moving sequentially from the generation and selection of items to the successful completion of a product.

12. The student will develop a more positive self-concept by recognizing and **using abilities**, becoming more **self-directed,** and **appreciating likenesses and differences** between himself and others.

13. The student will develop ideas related to **broad-based issues, themes, or problems.**

14. The student will be involved in an **in-depth learning experience** related to a self-directed topic.

15. The student will **generate original ideas** in completing a model, plan, picture, dance or other product that is unique.

16. The student will show an ability to recognize the goals and objectives of a group by **working toward consensus** in planned group activities.

17. The student will produce many pictures/movements to **make comparisons** among things, show relationships or associations.

18. The student will effectively **interpret** and use nonverbal forms of communication to express ideas, feelings, and needs to others.

19. The student will use a variety of pictures/movements to **describe feelings and values.**

20. The student will **predict** many different causes/effects of given situations through the use of pictures and movement.

21. The student will express a **variety** of kinds of responses. **(Flexibility)**

22. The student will express **unusual, uncommon** responses, though not all of the ideas prove to be useful. **(Originality)**

23. The student will **build onto or embellish** a basic idea by adding details to make it more interesting and complete. **(Elaboration)**

Products for Portfolios

a letter
a lesson
advertisement
annotated bibliography
art gallery
block picture story
collage
collection
chart
choral reading
comic strip
crossword puzzle
debate
demonstration
detailed illustration
diorama
display
editorial
essay
experiment
fact file
fairy tale
family tree
filmstrip
flip book
game
graph
hidden picture
illustrated story

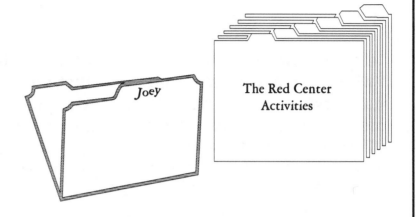

Joey

The Red Center
Activities

labeled diagram
large scale drawing
learning center
map
letter to the editor
map with legend
mobile
mural
museum exhibit
newspaper story
model
oral report
pamphlet
photo essay
pictures
picture story for children
poem
poster
project cube
puppet
puppet show
rebus story
science fiction story
sculpture
skit

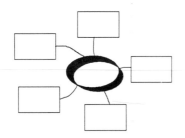

MindMapping

It's time for "True Confessions." Nancy Johnson hates outlines! (I wonder if Miss Westerlund knew that the outline for my senior research paper was written AFTER the paper was finished?) Organizing information, thoughts, and ideas into a sequential, linear pattern is tuff. Any why so many rules? You can't have a Roman numeral I without a II. You can't have a capital A without a B. What if you can't think of a B? Do you just forget about A? There is some comfort in knowing that outlining is difficult for lots of folks, both adult and child.

Have no fear, fellow outline haters! Help is on the way! It's called mindMapping. Adults may have a little difficulty adjusting to it at first, but take my word for it, kids will love it—from day one!

In her book, **It's About Writing** (Creative Learning Consultants, 1990), Kathy Balsamo says: "The process of mindMapping ideas stimulates the flow of thoughts to produce a written, verbal, abstract or concrete product. Organizing concepts in this manner is a VIABLE ALTERNATIVE TO OUTLINING." MindMapping as a physical process is visual; as a creative process it is intellectually manipulative. It can be visual, intellectual, AND kinesthetic if students have a physical way to move or manipulate parts of the mindMap. An easy way to do this is to provide students with multi-colored Post-It® note pads.

They can brainstorm their ideas, write them on the notes, stick them on their mindMaps, and then move the small pieces of self-adhesive paper around as they begin to organize their thoughts and ideas. If self-adhesive paper is cost prohibitive, use colored index cards, small pieces of colored construction paper, or colored memo cubed paper. Colored paper is much better than plain white. For schools with Mac computers, check out "*Inspiration*"—software by Ceres—a mindMapping program that allows for creative mindMapping followed by sequential outlining components.

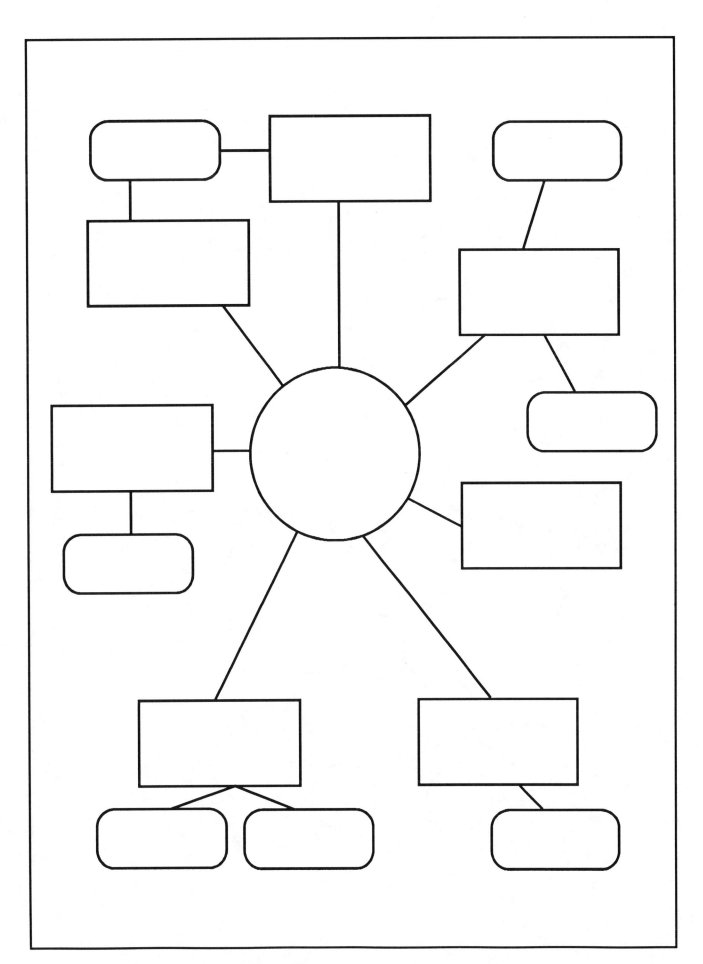

What are the Positive (+) and Negative (-) effects of your idea?

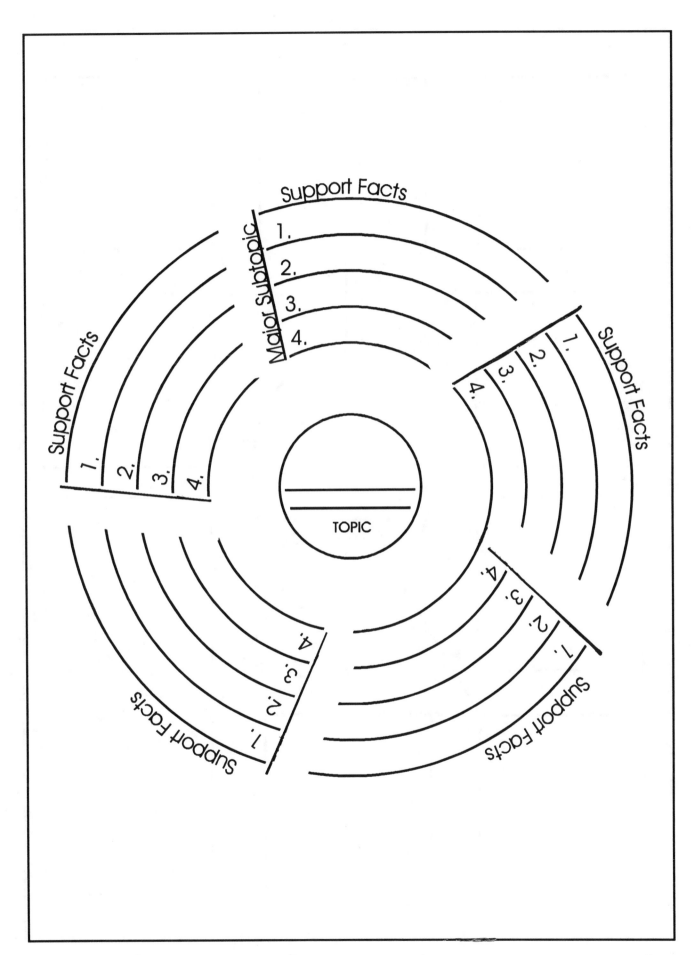

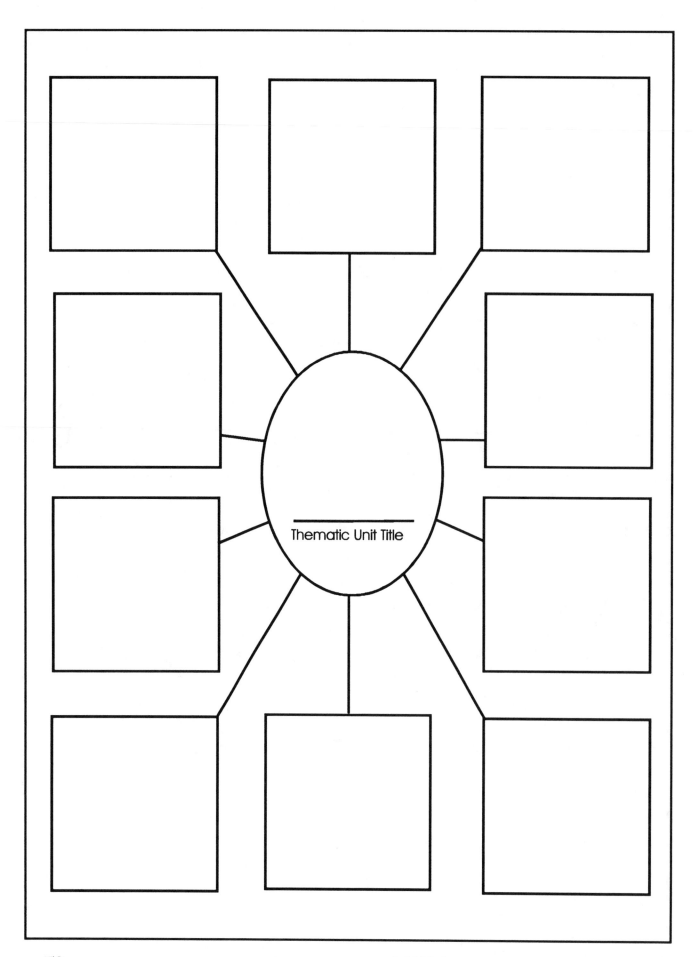

Thematic Unit Title

52

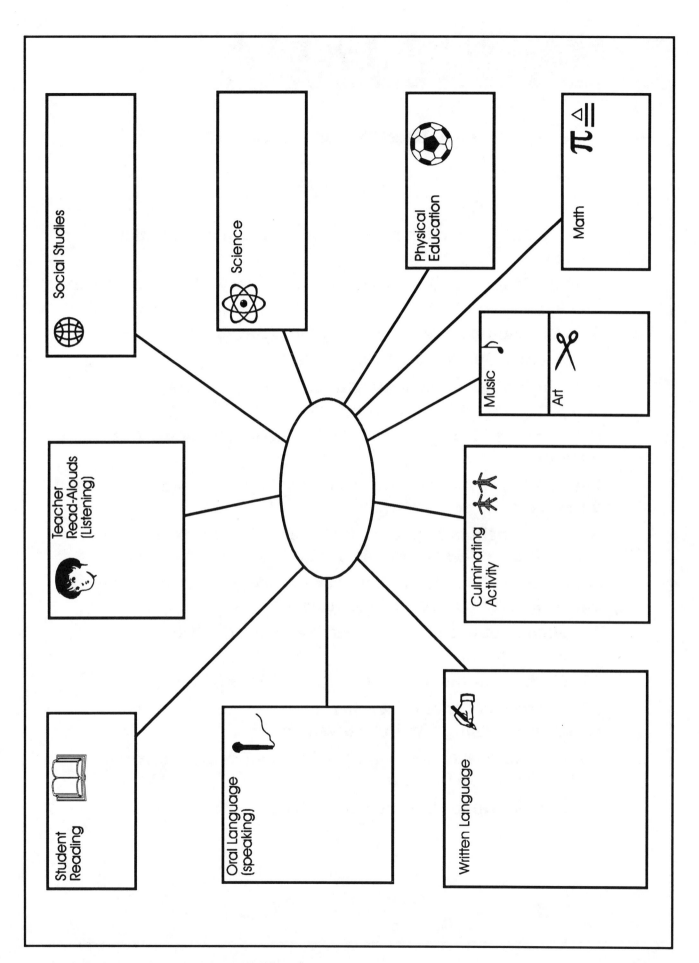

Social Studies

Science

Physical Education

Math

Music

Art

Teacher Read-Alouds (Listening)

Culminating Activity

Student Reading

Oral Language (speaking)

Written Language

Room Arrangements

Checklist

1. Is the library shelf in the front of the room and reading rug in the back?

2. Is the long, low shelf in front of the heater? Things will get a bit cool this winter!

3. Is the painting easel a long way from the sink?

4. Are noisy things like blocks on the rug?

5. Is there at least one writing table near a chalkboard, so kids can see to copy things from the board?

6. Where are the wall outlets? Did you cover them up with furniture?

7. Don't forget your pull-down screen. Is there room in front of it for everyone to see a movie?

8. Window light is important for some science experiments. It is best to have at least one table or shelf next to a window.

9. Do you really need all that board space? Cover some of it with paper, shelves, tables, or kids' artwork.

10. What about you? Did you leave a space that will be comfortable?

11. What about the fire code? Is there a safe path to the door?

12. Did you ask another teacher for advice? Someone else's experience might prove to be invaluable.

13. Have you asked the parents of your students for help in making furniture for your classroom?

14. Did you smile at the custodian today?

Nancy Johnson's Three-Year Room
Arrangement Progression A—H

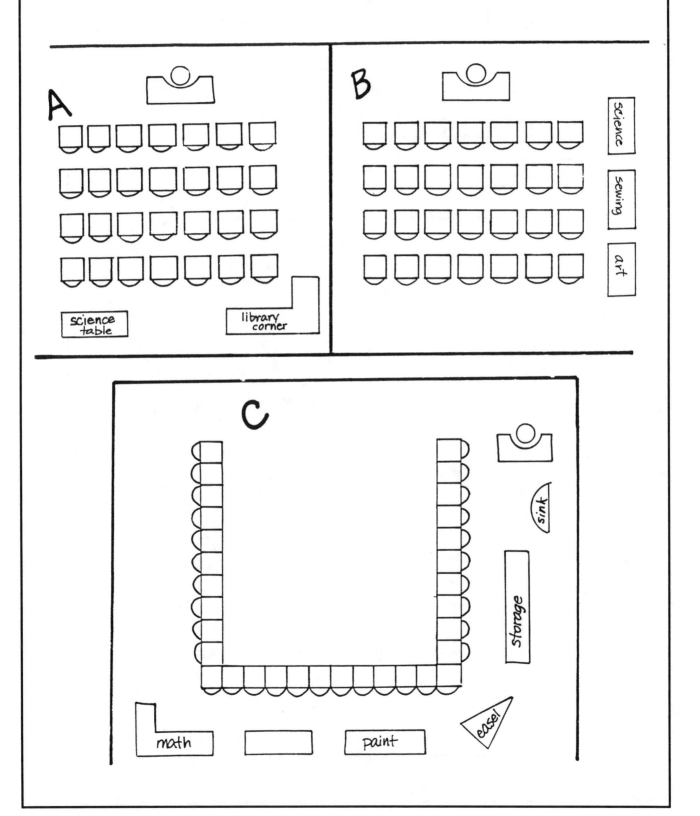

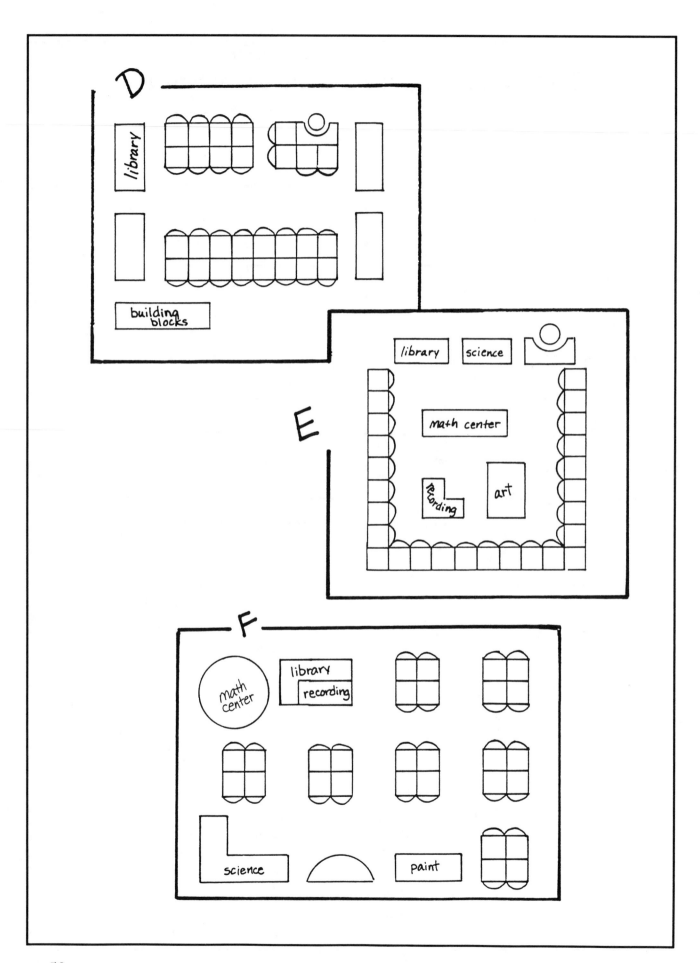

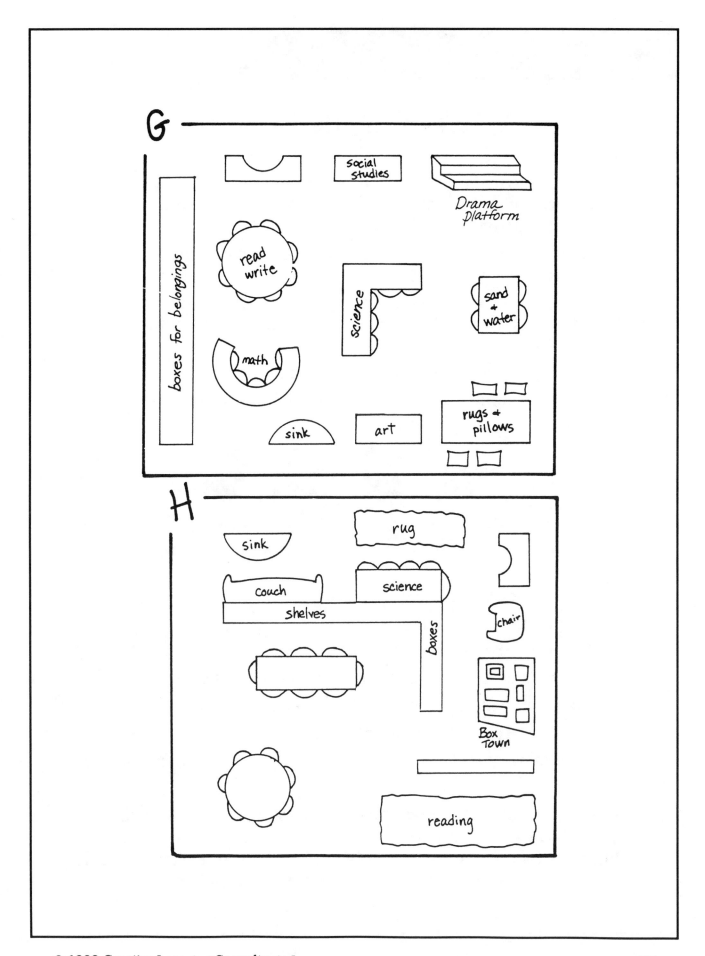

G

boxes for belongings

social studies

Drama Platform

read write

science

sand + water

math

sink

art

rugs + pillows

H

sink

rug

couch

science

shelves

boxes

chair

Box Town

reading

Learning Centers

The term *learning center* can be defined in many ways. It can be a physical area where the child engages independently in numerous, varied learning activities.

It can be a place where the child can learn something new in a certain content area.

Or a place where a child may assume responsibility for his own self-direction in choosing and carrying out a task and working at his own rate.

It can be an area where you send a child to carry out a task.

It can be a combination of the previously mentioned definitions.

Learning centers give the child opportunities

1. to practice making decisions
2. to practice following directions
3. to practice working independently
4. to practice new learnings and reinforce old learnings
5. to develop skills in working with other students
6. to learn from other students
7. to take responsibility for the use and care of materials.

Teachers using centers are able to work undisturbed with small groups or individuals and are able to circulate and observe pupils, gaining information about work habits, skills, attitudes, and observe learning processes for inclusion in assessment portfolios.

Children may profit most by using learning centers in the following situations:

    1. Assignment or choice during math or reading periods while the teacher works with small groups.

    2. Choice only after the child has completed instruction in a group or after completing assigned tasks.

    3. Assigned center during reading or math while teacher instructs other students in small groups or individually.

    4. "Learning Center Time" for 30 or 40 minutes for 2 to 5 days per week when all students work at one or more centers by choice and/or assignment. Some children might be assigned to get practice at a center with or without help for part of the time. Later, they might make a choice.

    5. Center activities for given topics in science or social studies for a period of two weeks or so at a time.

The Learning Center Checklist

1. What are my goals?

2. What activities will help in reaching my goals?

3. Can I work effectively and easily in a classroom with learning centers?

4. How many centers will I have?

5. Will I use desks, tables, or designated areas?

6. What types of material or equipment will I use?

7. How many children will be at each center at any one time?

8. How will I schedule the use of the centers?

9. How much guidance, if any, will be given?

10.What standards or goals will be expected from the students participating?

11. How will work be checked or evaluated?

12. How will cleanup be accomplished and by whom?

Getting Children to the Centers

Present alternatives to children so they may select one center which best fits their needs and interests. Some possibilities for scheduling are:

1. Morning meeting for class to discuss events, hand out needed materials and provide a time for children to sign up for various activities.

2. General activity block of time. While children work, the teacher meets with individuals or small groups of students.

3. Open choice. Children freely select learning activities and move from area to area with teacher assistance.

4. Student scheduling. Show various methods for children to record choices—flags, etc.

5. Daily class schedules. Teacher outlines schedule on chart or chalkboard and reviews the schedule with the children. She presents some type of signal to help them know when to change from one activity to another.

The Process

1. Develop:

Select a topic, subject, skill or interest as the basis for creating activities. Structure activities to include ways to receive information—listening, observing, experimenting, researching, and ways to apply information—making products, designing models, work sheets, puzzles, role playing, games, writing stories, matching objects.

2. Collect:

Locate all information about the topic, skill or area. Gather materials to be used for writing, drawing, building, modeling and sorting. Set up supplies.

3. Display:

Set up an area in the classroom. Arrange materials using tables, boxes, charts, bulletin boards, shelves, dividers, etc. Label items. Place directions in center. Allow for display of children's work.

4. Present:

Introduce activities. Give directions on how to use materials. Schedule times for using the center. Schedule individual conferences. Encourage students to act as teachers for the centers. Plan ways students can add activities.

5. Evaluate:

Develop a record-keeping instrument for students' or teacher's use. Provide ways for children to share products.

Assessment— Teacher Recording Instruments

Some types of record-keeping instruments for teachers are:

1. *Student portfolios.* Label a folder for each child. Use a sheet with date, observation, etc. to record information about the child. Use these folders for conferences with parents, pass on to other teachers, and for formal assessment.

2. *Index card file.* Label an index card for each child. Identify categories for different skill areas, needs and interests. The teacher writes notes about the child on his card and files this information for future use.

3. *Class chart.* Information regarding student activities may be recorded on a class chart. The information placed upon such a chart is limited if the chart is in view of the students.

Student Recording Instruments

Some types of record-keeping instruments for students are:

1. *Portfolios.* Students place student-chosen work based on criteria in content areas and products produced outside of school showing originality and the problem solving process in the portfolio. Samples can include audio-visual and computer products, written products such as first drafts and revised examples, and artwork and photographs of products. It may include logs and journals, reading lists for research completed, self-assessment, collaborative group work and products, and awards and honors.

2. *Treasure boxes.* Each child uses a box to keep the samples of work he treasures. The boxes can be shared during conferences. The teacher can add notes about the child's work to the box. This is a good method of recording for young children.

3. *Triangle notes.* The teacher provides large triangles with the words "Today some of my activities have been..." on it. The child can write in the remainder of the sentence. This record is sent home to parents at the end of the day. This method is time-consuming if students participate in several activities at centers.

4. *Picture records.* This method can be used by children or teachers. Take photographs of children at work or of projects they have completed. Place the pictures in a scrapbook. Write comments by the teacher and the child.

5. *Student letters.* Children are given copies of a letter to fill out at the end of the school day. They color in pictures of what they have done during the day or write about what they enjoyed most during the day's work. This method of evaluating encourages parent and student interaction.

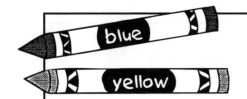

The "Red" Center

It's everywhere! Color that is. As an elementary teacher, I used color as a springboard for activities that developed thinking, reading, writing, and kinesthetic skills. One corner of the classroom was the "Color Corner" learning center. The ideas and activities that follow are from the Red Corner.

Resources/materials/supplies to be collected or prepared ahead of time:

"Red" art supply stuff (paint, markers, chalk, crayons, paper, collage materials)

List from library/media specialist of "red" stories, poems, nursery rhymes, trade books, films, videos, songs, etc. How about a storyteller?

Reproducible pages about the color red.

Students and teacher gather "bring-from-home" items that are different shades of red.

Talk to other teachers about ideas/help. Ask the P.E. teacher for a game that might use the color red.

Call the PTA president or parent volunteer and request a list of community resources. (theater groups, business/industry related to careers that use color, clubs/organizations) Parent volunteers can help organize a "Red Parade" or a "Red Food Lunch."

IDEAS

Decorate the "Color Corner" with bright red balloons, cutouts, and crepe paper.

Ask students to bring something red and wear something red. Categorize all the red stuff by size, shade, texture, smell, etc.

Play "Red Object Charades."

Have students make individual "Red Books."

Collect different shades of red cloth. Have students arrange the pieces by shade, lightest to darkest. Then use the pieces to create a collage or puppet.

Do a survey of students in other classrooms about their favorite color. Graph the results.

Place a few drops of red, yellow, and orange food coloring in bowls of water. Fold up sheets of paper towels and dip the corners and folds in the dye. Unfold and lay on newspaper to dry. Tape all the dry sheets together and hang the completed "Towel Quilt" on the wall. How many shades of red can you see and name in the quilt?

For more ideas, use the "Color Me Learning" chapter from **Thinking Is The Key**. (Creative Learning Consultants, 1992)

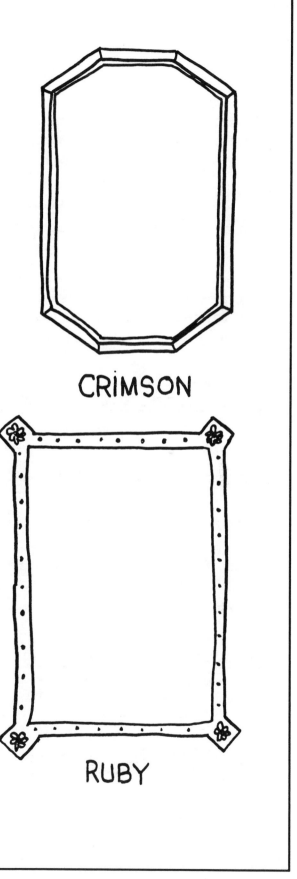

CRIMSON

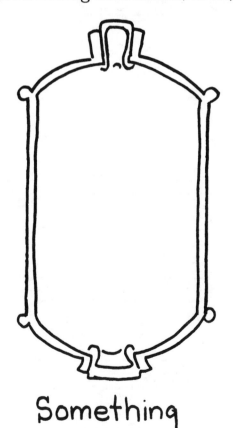

Something
SCARLET

RUBY

Recipe for Red

JOE WAYMAN

First you take a great big pot, a pot that holds an aw-ful lot.

Put it on a great big stove and heat it 'til it's nice and hot.

When you've done what I have said you'll end up with the col - or red.

Yes, of course, that's what I said, I have a re - ci - pe for red.

1. First you need the des - ert sun, crash of cym - bals more than one.

Blast of trum - pets for your ear,(a) ti - ny dash of sud - den fear.

Throw in sev - en signs for stop - ping, (a) rus - ty hatch - et tired of chop - ping,

Add a bad mo - squi - to bite, four - teen peo - ple in a fight.

(repeat to line 3)

It's getting closer don't you see, red's the color it will be,
It's not quite done of that I'm sure, I think it needs a little more.

2. A cup of sunny sunburned noses, three old worn-out fire hoses,
Add the fire engine too, a mean 'n nasty pirate crew.
A dash of fireworks from the sky, hot 'n spicy pepper pie.
A tiger in an iron cage, just a touch of purple rage.

It's getting closer don't you see, red's the color it will be,
It's not quite done of that I'm sure, I think it needs a little more.

3. A ladle full of broken bones, several large and ragged stones.
A last and lonely train caboose, a dragon prowling on the loose.
Stir in lots of summer heat, an August sidewalk for your feet
One explosion, not too big, an angry cat without its wig.

It's almost there, it's almost right, so let it boil through the night.
It isn't stew you'll have, instead,
Inside you'll find the color RED!

My very favorite color is:

A recipe for my color would go like this:

Recipe for _____.

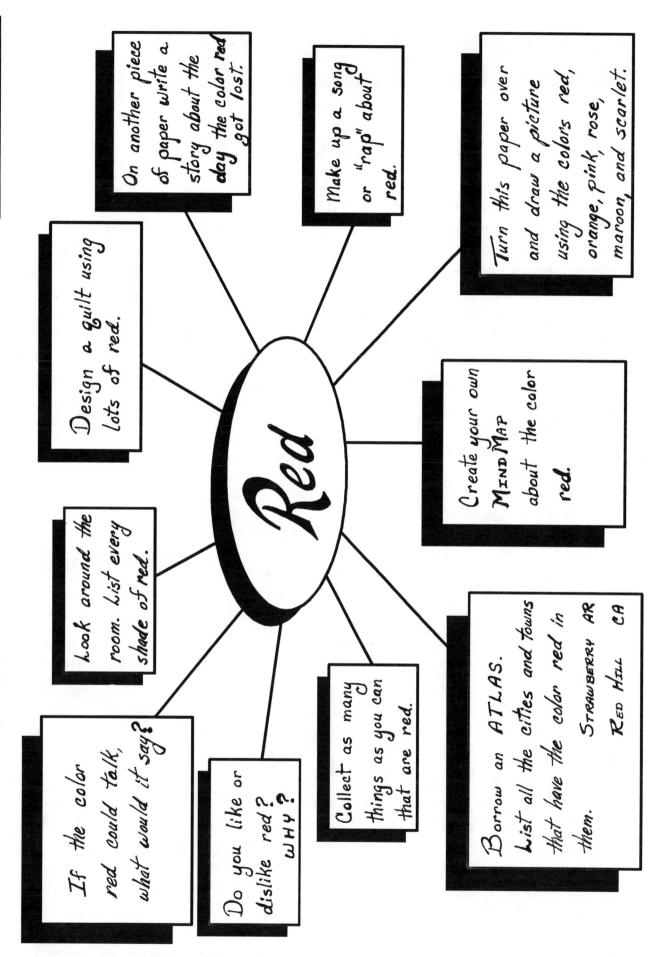

On another piece of paper write a story about the day the color red got lost.

Make up a song or "rap" about red.

Turn this paper over and draw a picture using the colors red, orange, pink, rose, maroon, and scarlet.

Design a quilt using lots of red.

Red

Create your own MIND MAP about the color red.

Look around the room. List every shade of red.

If the color red could talk, what would it say?

Do you like or dislike red? WHY?

Collect as many things as you can that are red.

Borrow an ATLAS. List all the cities and towns that have the color red in them.
STRAWBERRY AR
RED HILL CA

Cooperative Group Process

The experts are predicting ten job and three career changes for today's seventh graders as they enter the world of work in the 21st century. The only way to learn how to work with other people is to DO IT. Talking about cooperative learning, reading about it, or listening to someone give a speech about it won't result in much skill building. On the other hand, providing opportunities for students to role play the various behaviors required to work with other people is the first step in a life long process of learning how to be an effective co-worker and problem solver.

In a group situation several different behaviors reveal themselves as the group struggles to solve a problem. Some of the labels or terms for such behaviors are:

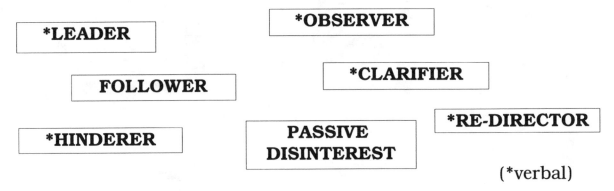

*LEADER	***OBSERVER**
FOLLOWER	***CLARIFIER**
*HINDERER **PASSIVE DISINTEREST**	***RE-DIRECTOR**

(*verbal)

After students have had several opportunities to work in small groups, begin a large group discussion which includes the definitions of the above roles. The leader, clarifier, and re-director are roles that require verbalization. The role of leader and follower should be discussed together. Good **leaders** understand how to follow and followers will not follow a leader they do not trust or understand.

Hinderers say and do things that have nothing to do with the group activity. **Observers** are visual learners, making comments related to visual details. **Clarifiers** are questioners. An effective leader uses clarifiers to get his message across to the followers. **Passively disinterested** group members do not lead, follow, hinder, or ask questions. They are like warm blobs taking up space in the universe! **Re-directors** are process oriented. They keep the group on task.

Organize students into small groups. Give each group member a small piece of paper that has one of the above roles written on it. They are not to show it to anyone. Give each group an activity or problem to solve. ("Blast Off!" is a good example.) Each group member is to role play what is written on their paper, exhibiting the appropriate behaviors.

At the end of the activity each group discusses what happened. Could they tell who was the **leader**? the **hinderer**? the **clarifier**? etc. How could they tell? Did they like playing that role? The teacher/facilitator mixes up the pieces of paper before the next group activity. By the end of the school year students should have had plenty of practice learning about the group process.

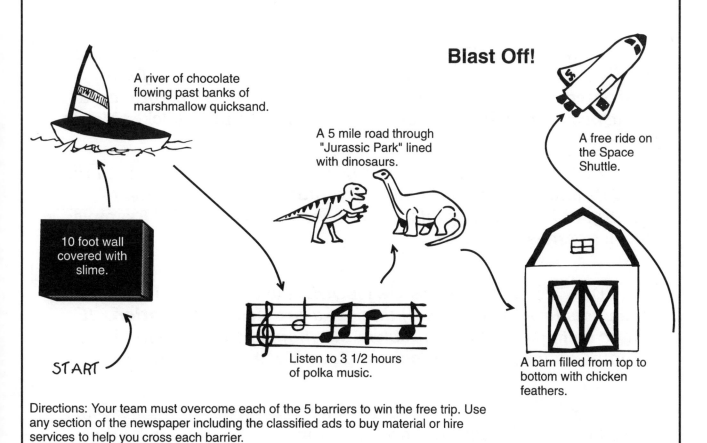

Blast Off!

A river of chocolate flowing past banks of marshmallow quicksand.

A 5 mile road through "Jurassic Park" lined with dinosaurs.

A free ride on the Space Shuttle.

10 foot wall covered with slime.

Listen to 3 1/2 hours of polka music.

A barn filled from top to bottom with chicken feathers.

START

Directions: Your team must overcome each of the 5 barriers to win the free trip. Use any section of the newspaper including the classified ads to buy material or hire services to help you cross each barrier.

Dot To Dot Stories

You've heard, "*Teacher, I don't know what to write about.*" But are your students **ready** to write? Use this activity to stimulate the imagination through kinesthetic thinking.

Buy a package of self-stick colored dots that includes at least three different colors. Stick one dot on the back of one hand of each student. Mix up the colors. Example: 1/3 of the class has red dots, 1/3 has blue, 1/3 has green. Ask the entire class to stand and get in groups of three (triads)—one blue dot, one red dot, and one green dot in each group. Ask each triad to find their own "space" so they can verbalize without interrupting others. The teacher gives the following verbal instructions to all the triads.

"*DON'T SAY ANYTHING OUT LOUD. Just think about my directions. All the blue dots (one in each triad) think of a name for a* **character**. *It could be a character from a book, a TV character, a comic book character, or one you make up.*" Example: Mickey Mouse

"*DON'T SAY ANYTHING OUT LOUD. Just think about it. All the red dots (one in each triad) think of a* **place**. *It can be a city, a country, or the corner of this room. It can be ANY PLACE.*" Example: Six Flags Amusement Park

"*DON'T SAY ANYTHING OUT LOUD. Just think about it. All the green dots (one in each triad) think of a* **problem or situation**. *It can be a simple, ordinary problem that happens in everyday life or it can be an imaginative problem.*" Example: A broken shoelace.

After a minute or two of "think time" the teacher continues with the following directions:"*The triad members share with each other the name of the character, place, and problem. Each triad begins to create a story that includes the character, place, and problem.*

After two or three minutes the teacher asks for a spokesperson from each triad to share their story with the rest of the class. After each story is heard, the teacher continues:

*"Remember what character, place, or problem **YOU** are. That does not change. Keep the same dot. Now all the blue dot people switch triads. (Go to a DIFFERENT triad.) When the blue dot gets to the new triad, the red and green dot people tell THEIR STORY. The new triad now ADDS the new character (blue dot) to the story and all three continue to create a story."*

Teacher asks for a spokesperson in each triad to share their story again with the new addition. This pattern of switching one dot, adding to the story, then telling the story again with the new additions is repeated several times. The stories get longer and longer as the groups add another character, another place, another problem, another character, etc. At some point, direct the students to go back to their seats and write a story. They can do this individually or with a partner. Some may choose to mindMap their ideas before writing.

Professional writers use this process. For them, a story consists of a place, a character, and a plot. In this case the word *problem* is substituted for *plot*. If the story isn't long enough add another character, add another place, add another problem. DOT TO DOT STORIES are a fun way for students to rid themselves of writer's block. It also gets them up off their backsides and makes storytelling and creative writing a learning by doing or kinesthetic process.

Note: The best activities are those you repeat. Do this activity several times, changing the premise or adding dots each time. Use four colors. The blues are characters, reds are places, greens are problems, and yellows are seasons of the year. Use four colors. Add emotions. Add careers.

See - Run - Do Posters!

This activity requires the integration of visual/kinesthetic thinking with strong communication skills. It is a flexible activity that can easily be adapted to fit different grade levels or subject areas. Best of all, it's lots of fun! The object of the activity is for each group to construct a poster that looks like the sample poster.

Teacher Pre-Activity

Construct a sample **See-Run-Do** poster to use during the group activity. Do NOT let students see the poster.

Materials: markers, scissors, glue, tape, construction paper, newspaper, and various collage materials.

Construction: Use standard size white poster board. The sample poster might have a theme such as a season, holiday, famous person, or event. Or construct a poster that is not limited to one theme. Provide a simple poster the first time. The pictured poster is an example of a poster not limited to one idea.

Procedure: Draw two-dimensional shapes, symbols, animals on the poster board. Glue a three-dimensional shape such as a cylinder or construction paper tube on the poster. Cut newspapers into silhouette shapes representing clouds and buildings. Glue them to the poster. Glue other collage materials to the poster (feathers, pipe cleaners, crepe paper, pasta, etc.)

Student Activity

Assign students to groups of six or seven. Ask each group to select two VERY VERBAL people. (Teacher may assign students.) One will be the **DESCRIBER.** The other will be the **RUNNER.**

Provide materials for other group members to choose from. Include the same materials the teacher used to construct the sample **See-Run-Do** poster.

THE DESCRIBER: Hang the sample poster outside the classroom. Describers remain outside the classroom during the entire activity. Only the describers may look at the sample poster. NO ONE ELSE SEES IT UNTIL THE ACTIVITY IS COMPLETELY OVER! After a describer looks at the sample poster, he moves away from the poster to a pre-determined spot outside the classroom to talk to his runner. He describes the poster to the runner. The describers may look at the sample poster as many times as they want. The describers may not see the poster their group is constructing until the end of the activity.

THE RUNNER: The runner returns to the classroom and communicates the describer's description of the poster to his/her group. Because he did not see the sample poster, he must rely on his describer to give him the details he needs to relay an accurate description to the group. The runner may make as many trips as he wishes. The runner may NOT touch any group materials or use his hands when he returns to talk to the group. Each group of poster makers may ask their runner as many questions as they want. Time limit: 20-30 minutes.

Follow Up: After the time limit expires, gather all the describers, runners, and poster makers together. Compare/contrast the posters from each group with the sample poster. Process the entire activity by asking the students to reflect on their feelings.

Questions to consider: How did the runners communicate without using their hands? Was it easier being a describer, runner, or poster maker? How did the time limit affect the activity?

Bears in the Bag!

Students learn best by DOING. They must be physically, emotionally, and intellectually involved in the learning process. The teacher must integrate content so that students are learning abstractly and concretely. Through the use of divergent questions "Bears in the Bag!" invites the learner to move, imagine, interact and problem solve.

Ask students to bring a TEDDY BEAR to class hidden in a paper bag. Encourage them to keep the sacks closed. (It's a secret!) Mix up the sacks so students do not have their own. Organize students in partners. In each partnership one student is number one and the other number two. Proceed with the following instructions:

"Number ones, reach in the sack you are holding. Don't look! Just touch. Give your partner one word descriptions of what you feel. Don't name the kind of bear, just describe it."

"Number twos, look in your sack. Tell your partner all the things the bear might say if it could talk."

"Number ones, 'heft' your sack and complete the following statements for your partner: It feels heavier than a ...   It feels lighter than a ..."

Ask all the ones and twos to write words all over the sacks that describe the stuffed bear. (Don't look inside yet!) Have students switch sacks. Have students read all the words written on the sack and draw a picture of the stuffed bear he thinks is inside. When each student is finished, he shows his drawing to the owner of the bag, opens it and takes out the bear. Did the stuffed bear and the drawings look alike? How close were they? Which details were correct or incorrect?

Ask students to exchange sacks and bears until they get their own. Organize students into partners and ones and twos. Ones and twos take turns responding to the following:

Introduce your bear to your partner.

What is your bear's name?

When did you get it?

Who gave it to you? Why?

Compare and contrast the two bears.

If your teddy bear is a friend, what qualities does it have that real friends don't have?

What kind of feelings do you share with your teddy bear?

Does your teddy bear always agree with your opinions?

What does it mean to "*grin and bear*" it?

Compare/contrast your bear to a real bear.

Compare/contrast your bear to a doll.

What are all the things your bear could be besides a stuffed toy?

What are all the materials that went in to making your bear?

How would your bear feel about bear traps?

Compose a list of questions a real bear might ask a bear hunter.

Stand up and give your partner a bear hug.

Give your bear a personality. Pretend your bear can talk. How would it answer the following questions:

What is your favorite color?

Favorite food?

Are you a talented bear?

Do you go to bear school?

Favorite musical group?

WHAT IF...

      your teddy bear had lights on it?

      your teddy bear had roller skates?

      your teddy bear could change color?

      owning a teddy bear was against the law?

Do you have lots of friends? Who are they?

What are you going to be when you grow up?

What one thing really bugs you about humans?

Would you rather be a real bear? Why? or Why not?

Teddy Bear

by Joe Wayman

I first saw him sitting there,
A great big fat and furry bear.
Bright and shiny button nose,
Yellow zippers, boots and bows.

I knew at once he had to be,
A Teddy Bear meant just for me.
I picked him up, he seemed to fit,
He snuggled 'neath my chin a bit.

That Teddy Bear came home with me,
And sometimes sits upon my knee.
I bump him sometimes on his head,
And thump him till he must be dead.

I snuggle him and huggle him.
He's always there through thick and thin.
My friend when I have messed up bad.
My friend when I am sad or glad.

When I fall and skin my knee.
He's always waiting there for me.
When I need a special friend,
He sits beside me till the end.

The world is filled with pain and care,
And when there's sorrow I must share,
I'll make it though 'cause he is there,
Teddy Bear, my Teddy Bear.

And when he's gone and lost his hair,
And when his fuzz is almost bare,
I'll love him then, yes, I'll still care,
Teddy Bear, my Teddy Bear.

The *PULGAR*

The Pulgar originated with Larry Weatherford from southern Illinois. The basis of this activity is a story told or read by the teacher / facilitator. The version that follows can easily be expanded or altered to fit the situation as well as the talents of the storyteller.

The word **Pulgar** is an invented word that doesn't mean anything. When the listeners hear the word and the story, they are encouraged to form their own unique ideas or images of the "creature."

During the telling/reading of the story, the teacher/facilitator should NOT use specific words to describe the physical features of the **Pulgar**. Examples of words to avoid—*foot, feet, claws, teeth, hairy, scales, tail, paws, hands, arms, ears.* The listeners are encouraged to form their own conclusions about what the **Pulgar** really looks like.

The story describes what the **Pulgar** DOES—not what it looks like. During the telling of the story the teacher/facilitator uses many words to describe what the **Pulgar** is DOING. Examples—*walking, dragging, pulling, eating, chomping, biting, grabbing.* The listeners form mental images of the **Pulgar's** activities and use them to construct their own version of the creature.

The teacher/facilitator prepares **PULGAR KITS** ahead of time—one Kit for each group of five to eight students. Fill a large manila envelope or paper sack with ONE each of the following items: scissors, tape, bottle of glue, and marker. *(Note: There is only one item of each kind in a Kit to force group members to share and cooperate during the construction of the **Pulgar**.)* In addition to those items, **Pulgar Kits** might include the following: balloons, newspaper, yarn, cotton balls, construction paper, paper plates, stickers, straws, etc. Actually, you can put almost any kind of "artsy/craftsy" stuff in **Pulgar Kits**! (**Pulgar Kits** are a good excuse for cleaning out the scrap box or your own desk!)

IMPORTANT POINT: Each Kit must have the **SAME** "stuff", **SAME** amount. One of the purposes of the activity is to show students how one set of materials can produce many results.

DO NOT HAND OUT THE *PULGAR* KITS UNTIL AFTER THE STORY HAS BEEN TOLD

Group participants in clusters of five to eight, sitting around tables or on the floor in a circle. The teller/reader of the **Pulgar** story is encouraged to add, change, or improve on the story. Be creative! Let your imagination pull you into the story.

You can soften the lights in the room to create a quiet, calm mood for the telling/reading of the story. You can add a fan or turn the air conditioning WAY down. Or you can tell the story inside the BUBBLE (see page **87**).

The *PULGAR* Story

"Make yourself as comfortable as possible. Relax. Be calm and quiet. Close your eyes if you wish. I'm going to tell you a story. Try to create pictures in your mind as I tell the following story.

"It is wintertime and the weather is COLD. Very COLD. You are all bundled up in a heavy snowsuit, fur-lined boots, mittens, and hat. You are hiking in the mountains. And you are all alone. The air is sharp and crisp. There is a heavy blanket of snow on the ground. It is so cold your boots make a squeaking, crunching sound as you press them into the snow. You can see your breath as you hike higher and higher up into the mountains. Your cheeks are red and sting from the cold. The air smells fresh, filled with the scent of pine. Your backpack seems to get heavier and heavier as the mountain air gets thinner and thinner.

"As you climb, you pass rocks, pine trees, and drifts of snow. You hear a wolf howl in the distance. The sound of your heavy boots frightens a rabbit just to your left. Your cold nose can just barely smell the scent of pine. Higher and higher you climb until you pass the tree line. You realize that from this point on there will be no more trees, only snow, rocks, and an occasional bare patch of ground. Still you climb, higher and higher—breathing harder and harder. Your body is feeling so tired and heavy. You must find a place to rest. Your eyes spot the entrance to a cave. It looks so warm and inviting. You crawl inside and pull off your heavy backpack. The cave feels warm and cozy as you curl up for a much needed nap.

"Suddenly you are awakened by a sound that is coming from deep inside the cave. You are frightened by the strangeness of the sound. And just like the rabbit you saw earlier, you scurry outside dropping your backpack behind you. Your curiosity forces you to hang back, close by the entrance of the cave. Whatever is inside is slowly moving its way out of the cave. And then you remember

*what day it is. You realize what is making the noise. Of course! What else could it be? It must be **THE PULGAR!!!***

"A **Pulgar** is a very special creature. It sleeps in a cave all year long except for ONE DAY. On one particular day each year, the **Pulgar** is allowed to leave its cave to do just ONE THING. EAT!!! And wouldn't you know it—this is the day. The **Pulgar** has to eat as much as it can in one day. You watch the **Pulgar** pull itself out of the cave. It stretches and yawns from its long sleep. It quickly feels its hunger. It scoops up a big mouthful of snow. As it heads away from its cave it begins to eat its way down the mountain. You are careful to stay at a safe distance, but once again your curiosity forces you to follow the **Pulgar.**

"As the **Pulgar** reaches the tree line, it chomps on a pine tree, pine cones and all. It eats rocks and dirt and snow. It chases after the rabbit you saw earlier. A fox jumps from behind a rock and the **Pulgar** takes after it. The **Pulgar** is like an eating machine. Eating more and more. Always eating. When it gets to the valley at the base of the mountain, it heads into a small village. There are no people to be seen anywhere. They know what day it is! The **Pulgar** eats a mailbox, a piece of sidewalk and the wheel of a mini van. It eats and eats and eats!!!

"As the day wears on the **Pulgar** can feel itself getting fuller and fuller, but it must not stop eating. It knows that it will be another whole year before it has a chance to eat again. The **Pulgar** leaves a path of destruction through the village as it heads back up the mountain. It must be back in its cave before the day is over. Still it eats more and more. Just one more tree, one more pine cone, one more mouth of snow. The **Pulgar** is so full it can hardly move. It drags and pulls itself back up the mountain, above the tree line, and back into its cave. It circles three times—round and round and round, burps twice, and lays down in a heap, ready to sleep its long sleep. Dreams of the next **Pulgar Day** dance in its head.

*"You may open your eyes. Please stay in your groups, but do not talk. I am going to give each group a **PULGAR KIT.** Without talking, each group is to make—construct—build—a **Pulgar** using the materials in the Kit. Remember! **DON'T TALK!**"*

Note: The entire construction may be done non-verbally. However, I usually start the construction non-verbally and about half way through tell them they may start talking and finish their **Pulgar** verbally.

Note 2: On most occasions, groups will construct their **Pulgar** using all or most of the materials in the Kit. (The balloons are important Kit items because they make a good base or foundation for the **Pulgar**.) However, once in awhile a group will use one of its members as a **Pulgar** and decorate him/her with the items from the Kit. (It's called risk taking!)

Allow about 15 minutes for construction. The teacher/facilitator then says:

*"As you finish constructing your **Pulgar,** create a name for it. Talk about its personality. Choose a group member to be a spokesperson. They will share the information later with the other groups. They must be prepared to explain what the various parts of the **Pulgar** mean."*

Have A **Pulgar Parade!** Take Pictures! Call The Newspaper! Write Stories!

As you were listening to the story, how did you "picture" the **Pulgar** in your mind? Where would your **Pulgar** like to go on vacation? Did your group's **Pulgar** turn out the way you imagined it during the story?

How did it feel to not be able to talk? There were not enough supplies for each person to have his own. How did you share materials? How did you communicate?

Feather Day

It was 8 AM on April Fool's Day. The principal announced over the intercom that ALL teachers were to report to the office immediately.

One of my students said, "*Oh, goodie! They're all in trouble! What did you do, Miss Johnson?*" With a shrug of my shoulders I headed down the hall. Maybe there was a tornado coming. Maybe war had been declared. Maybe somebody died. Whatever it was, it was the first time we had all been called to the office at the same time.

As we gathered in the office, our faces reflecting confusion and concern, the principal gave each of us a bag of feathers—several different colors, shapes, and sizes. As we peered into the bags, the principal proceeded with the following directions:

"*Congratulations! Today is going to be* **FEATHER DAY** *at Jefferson School. I want you to take this bag of feathers back to your classrooms and teach with them all day. Teach whatever subject or lesson you had planned—just make sure you use feathers.*

"*You may team teach, change the* schedule, use the library, go outside, or raid the supply closet. Let your creativity and imagination be your guide. I want to see reading, language arts, math, science, social studies, music, art, and P.E. taught with FEATHERS!

"By the way, there are three things you may NOT use today. I'm going to announce the three things over the intercom and tell all the students. That way if anyone cheats, the students are to come to the office and report them! You may not use textbooks, workbooks, or worksheets in any way, shape or form." (When he said no worksheets he was looking right at me. I was the "*Ditto Queen*" of the building!)

Most of the teachers stared in disbelief at the feathers and then the principal. The reactions were varied, to say the least. Fred Jenkins who had taught 6th grade for a hundred years looked very pale. Miss Gibson, the kindergarten teacher, started jumping up and down exclaiming, "*Wow! This is neat! What a great idea!*" She immediately ran down the hall toward her classroom. (Kindergarten teachers are a little different!) Second grade teacher, Mary Smith, leaned over and whispered in my ear, "Maybe we should call the principal's wife. I think he's gone crazy."

Finally, the principal said, "*Ok, get on with it. Get back to your classrooms and teach with those feathers. Have a good day!*"

So began a day of creativity, stretching, and risk taking for teachers and students at Jefferson School. We counted, sorted, and measured feathers. (It was 85 red feathers from the water fountain to the door!) We wrote stories, drew pictures, and researched birds and feathers. We floated them in the air and had feather races. We composed feather poems and songs. We took imaginary rides on our feathers. We took surveys to find out which color was the favorite. (Pink won!) We composed a list of questions that a wing feather on an eagle might ask a scale on a salmon. The fourth grade wrote a radio mystery entitled "*The Case of the Missing Feather Pillow.*"

At noon about half of the teachers showed up in the lunch room with a pencil and notebook ready to copy down ideas from each other.

Feather Day ended with a staff meeting in the library. When asked by the principal about the day's events, the teacher's comments included:

"*What a fun day! Can we do it next year?*"

"*I thought it was stupid. I had my lesson plans done for today. I know I don't always have them done, but today I did! Of course I couldn't use them. I had to use those dumb feathers! We aren't going to do this again next year are we?*"

"*I did all right. I never realized there were so many things you could do with feathers.*"

"*You took away the tools of my trade—my textbooks, my workbooks, and my dittos! I got so desperate, I asked the kids for ideas!*"

Miss Gibson showed up in a feather costume her kindergarten class had glued on her.

Mrs. Anderson had a glazed look in her eyes. Blinking slowly, speech a bit slurred, she said, "*Well I was a little nervous in the morning. I wasn't sure I would be able to think of things to do. By noon I had taken two Valium so the afternoon was fine!*"

The staff meeting ended with the principal saying:

"*Today you taught with feathers. If you can teach with feathers, you can teach with anything! Today you used the most important teaching tool you have—**your own creativity.***

hen our students at Jefferson School get through with the great educa-tion experience in this country there aren't going to be any textbooks, workbooks, or dittos. There might be feathers. There surely will be the need for creativity. Our students need us to **MODEL creativity.** *That's what you did today. You are the best teachers in the district. I'm proud of you."*

The Feather Day saga continued every April Fool's Day. Except each year the principal surprised his staff with something different. Over the years he gave each teacher a jar of peanut butter, a bowl with two fish in it, a bunch of bananas, a sack full of rocks that he and his wife had col-lected on a trip out west, and a box full of ribbon, string, cord, and twine that he collected from a textile factory. Oh, yes, and there were the water-melons!

Each April Fool's Day the directions were the same. *"Teach with this all day. No textbooks, no workbooks, no worksheets."* And every April Fool's Day at Jefferson School the most important teaching tool—**CREA-TIVITY**—was modeled and used for a group of very lucky students.

How to Build The *Bubble*

*The **Bubble** idea originated with Larry Weatherford from southern Illinois. It was expanded upon by Joe Wayman and then with thousands of teachers in the 1970s, 80s, and today.*

The **Bubble** is extremely simple to build and many are in use in schools throughout the United States. Teachers and children are building them and using them in many ways. How to do it? It's easy!

From a lumber or building supply store buy 4-mil painters' plastic. Buy it large enough so that you can cut a piece of it 12 feet by 24 feet.

Fold the sheet in half so that you have a double thickness 12 feet square.

Seal the three open sides with duct tape. Don't worry, it need not be air tight. In fact, you may choose to put four or five small holes in what will be the top of the Bubble.

Make a six-foot cylindrical tube from the remaining plastic that will fit around a large portable window fan (much like the tube that ran from the house in "**E.T.**")

Cut a slit in one end of the **Bubble** and tape the tube to it.

In the end of the cylindrical tube farthest from the Bubble, place the fan. Tape the plastic to the fan.

Cut a slit for a door in the end of the **Bubble** opposite the tube. Reinforce the slit with duct tape to keep it from tearing.

Your **Bubble** is now complete and will comfortably accommodate up to 15 people at a time.

Turn on the fan and the **Bubble** will inflate, usually in less than three minutes.

Images can be projected onto the surface of the **Bubble** using 16mm projectors, slide projectors, overheads, etc. The translucent plastic acts as a rear projection screen, and the images are visible and come alive on the inside.

Using several projected images at a time, the entire surface of the **Bubble** can be covered with images. The effect on the inside is that of stepping into another world—the world of your choice. What it is and where you go with it is only limited by your own imagination.

The inside of the **Bubble** can be decorated to fit a holiday theme; a book setting (the underground magic kingdom of **Alice in Wonderland**); a science environment (the sea with seaweed coming up from the floor or down from the ceiling with varieties of fish "floating" by thread from the top; outer space with aluminum stars hanging from the top and the outside of the **Bubble** covered with a piece of black plastic).

The **Bubble** can be used inside or outside in the classroom, in the hallway, in an open field, in the gym.

The **Bubble** can also take different shapes. One of the first **Bubbles** was a human heart with four chambers. As students "toured" the four chambers, they listened to a taped message of the workings of the chamber and heard the constant thumping of the blood and valves.

The uses of the **Bubble** are only limited by teacher and student imagination.

— Joe Wayman

Using the *Bubble* in the Classroom

The BUBBLE is an inflatable environment. In fact, it is a large balloon to climb into and pretend you are somewhere "out of this world." The Bubble obliterates your familiar world, and as you climb into it, reality is left behind and the world of imagination takes its place. Once inside, planned media experiences are projected on its surface to totally surround and involve the participant/observer. It becomes impossible to remain inert; one is forced to become involved.

The purpose of the Bubble is to create a total environment where learning can take place through the utilization of all the senses. The Bubble completely surrounds the individual with not only visual experience, but incorporates sound, touch and smell. The effect on the inside is one of being swept away to another time, another place. Images totally encompass you, happening simultaneously on all sides and around you.

Experience extends from visual to sound to touch to smell to visual, continually changing as the senses are aroused and the individual becomes totally involved. The interior becomes a physical environment using props: objects to touch, feel, smell and taste. Sound surrounds you being amplified from the outside, and due to the unique acoustics of the interior, the sound seems to flow throughout the Bubble, engulfing it from every direction.

Through the stimulation of as many senses as possible simultaneously the mind, body and emotions are caught up and become involved in a media/experience in learning.

You can be in your own classroom one minute, step into the Bubble, and in seconds be deep in space, under the sea, inside a single drop of water, an atom, or on a mountain top. Or you can experience what it would be like to be an orange, a pig, or French chef. The sensory impressions which can be created in the Bubble are as limitless as the imaginations of the people "programming" it.

90

How it Works

The following description of a sample activity using "The Sea" as a theme is only one idea of how the Bubble can be used. You are encouraged to use no prescribed format, follow no one's rigid pattern with the Bubble, but let yourself go, let your kids go, turn on your imagination and the Bubble will be a unique media/learning experience for both you and your students.

The Sea

"Relax...Everyone sit back...I am going to take you on a trip through your imagination. Clear your mind...Open your "inner" eyes and take a walk with me...You are on the beach...It is late afternoon and the sound of the waves comes to you across the empty expanse of the beach...deserted... silent...soft salt spray...The sun hangs over the sea...drifting slowly down. Gulls hang and swoop balanced first against the breeze then wheeling down to touch the surface of the water. As you walk, kick off your shoes...Feel the sand between your toes. You are totally alone. Free...And the sea is whispering to you...Reach down and roll up your pant legs as you walk... What do you see...Smell the salt...The waves are crashing down on the sand and roll up to you, sometimes catching your feet. The water feels cold at first but as you walk, you let the tide get deeper—to your ankles, calves, and up to your knees. Now you are facing the sea. After the heat of the day, the water is cool and inviting on your body...You are going to dive into the water ...Now I want you all to stand, open your eyes, and follow me into the sea."

(In subdued light students remove shoes and enter the Bubble.)

"It is totally dark. You feel softness beneath your feet and hear the sloshy rustle of seaweed caught in gentle currents. You are sitting on a soft floor; the floor of the sea. In the distance comes the sound of a gentle music of the sea. From out of the blackness comes a gentle voice. 'The sea is my friend,' it says. And as the music gathers in intensity you are slowly bathed in blue-green light. Seaweed sways and glitters in the soft green world as it stretches toward the surface. Soft blue sea anemones float lazily all around you, above

and on all sides large and small fish swim in lazy patterns. Suddenly, over your shoulder an octopus comes coyly out of the rocks and a school of seahorses scuttles by. The music seems to gather force and half of your world is suddenly in watery tumult. The water crashes down in giant whirlpools taking you headlong into the maelstrom. Now it calms, the fish return and the mood grows gentle. You are floating again. Now the sea world is growing dark and you are plunged back into blackness. . ."

After several seconds or minutes depending upon group responses, the leader indicates the door and steps out of the BUBBLE. You blink as you step back into reality. You have been to the bottom of the sea and back again.

—*by Joe Wayman*

Puzzling Activities

Study it—contemplate the meaning—re-draw it—color it—expand it—infuse it into your curriculum. And, when you are finished, post it in the teachers' lounge, hang it on your wall, duplicate it for students, frame it for your home.

Self Knowledge Activity

Have students write the word **"ME"** in the center piece of the puzzle. Have them separate the puzzle pieces. Then have students look at their disassembled puzzle. Discuss the **"ME"** piece.

a) Why is it separate?

b) How did it fall out?

c) Who will put it back?

d) What if it won't fit?

e) Who is **"Me?"**

f) How does **"Me"** feel?

g) What good is the puzzle without **"Me?"**

Have students fill in the other puzzle pieces with words, numbers, symbols, designs, colors or pictures that can be related to their concept of **"Me."**

Cross Curriculum Activities

HISTORY Have students fill in the pieces with events, places or things associated with an historical event. Have each student become a person in history—the **"ME"** in the puzzle. Ask them to explain who they are, how they got there, what part they played, how they are related to other pieces of the puzzle, and if they had behaved differently, how history may have been changed.

SELF-ESTEEM Duplicate a puzzle for each student. Have students fill in the puzzle pieces with positive feelings and characteristics. Have them create a puppet, write a story or poem (their choice) about the **"ME"** piece and how it relates to the pieces of the puzzle.

CAREER PUZZLE Duplicate a puzzle for each student. Have each student fill in each puzzle piece with things that they like to do. In small groups, brainstorm five occupations each student could do combining all of their "likes."

HAVE A "PUZZLE DAY" Have students bring in favorite puzzles. Time different age students putting different sized puzzles together. Calculate the average time it takes to put together a 100 piece puzzle, 500 piece puzzle, 1000 piece puzzle. Critique commercial puzzles making recommendations for different age groups. Study letter writing and how to give constructive criticism. Then submit recommendations to the manufacturer.

IMPORTANT PEOPLE I HAVE KNOWN Use the puzzle to make students aware of the important people in their lives and how individuals are influenced by others. Have them fill in as many pieces as possible with their favorite people— Grandma Joy, cousin Bill, sister Janie, teacher, coach, and baby-sitter. Write a word in each piece that tells how the person has been an influence.

ASSIGNMENT PUZZLE Use the puzzle pieces to record daily assignments. Color them upon completion of the assignment.

PROJECT PUZZLE Record parts of a project and the dates due on each piece. Cut the puzzle apart. Add a piece as different parts of the project become due—rough draft, note cards, bibliography, outline, and visuals. The Project is complete when the puzzle is complete.

LITERATURE PUZZLE Each puzzle piece becomes a character out of the literature being read. Have students identify each character, giving personality, physical description and purpose in the story. Cut each puzzle apart. Divide into small groups. Have each group pick two puzzle pieces out of a grab bag. Compare the characteristics of each character and discuss how the story might have ended differently if the characters exchanged roles in the story. If the "ME" piece is chosen, the group develops a new character and rewrites the ending adding the **"ME"** character to the story.

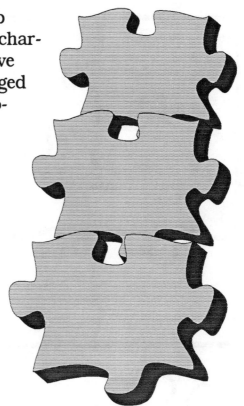

MATH Give each puzzle piece a number. Have students calculate the sum or product of all the numbers. Have students add, subtract, divide and multiply pieces. Ask students to generate math problems by combining puzzle pieces in different ways. How many math problems can they create with fourteen puzzle pieces?

VISIT A PUZZLE MAKING FACTORY Study puzzles from all aspects: product development, design, art, math needed to create, advertising, production cost, creating the machines to develop the puzzles, and cost.

ENVIRONMENTALLY PUZZLED Challenge students to study one environmental issue and create a puzzle that will teach others about the problem and what they can do to help.

To create your own puzzle activities, you can find puzzles in your local teacher supply store or order the *9-Piece Student Puzzle (4" x 5 1/2" blank puzzles—Pack of 20 9-piece pastel puzzles—$5.00 plus $3.00 shipping)* from *Pieces of Learning*—Beavercreek, Ohio.

96

Recognizing the Value of
All Contributions

The Bank Robbery

You may organize yourselves in any way you like. Each of the pieces of paper I'm holding (Clues listed on the next page) contains one clue that will help you solve a bank robbery. If you put all the facts together, you will be able to solve the mystery. However, you must determine which clues are valid. Your job is to find the robber. Any time you think you know the answer and the group agrees on the guess you may tell me. Time allotment is 20-30 minutes.

From time to time the facilitator may restate the title, emphasizing the value of ALL contributions.

—Source for Mysteries: Area Service Center for Gifted, Carthage, Illinois

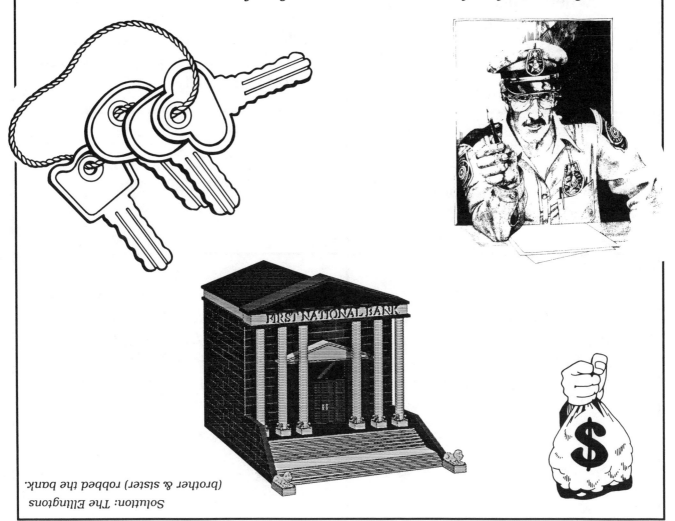

Solution: The Ellingtons (brother & sister) robbed the bank.

Miss Margaret Ellington, a teller at the bank, discovered the robbery.	Mr. Smith was found by the FBI in Dogwalk, Georgia, on November 12. He had arrived there via Southern Airlines Flight 414 at 5:00 pm on the 11th.
The front door of the bank had been opened with a key.	The president of the bank had been having trouble with his wife who spent all of his money. He had frequently talked of leaving her.
Miss Ellington said that Smith had often flirted with her.	There were no planes out of Dogwalk between 4:00 pm and 7:00 am.
When police tried to locate the janitor of the bank, Elwood Smith, he had apparently disappeared.	Mr. Greenbags waited in the terminal at O'Hare Field in Chicago for 16 hours because of engine trouble on the plane he was to take to Mexico City.
A substantial amount of dynamite had been stolen from Acme Construction Company on Wednesday, November 10.	The airline clerk confirmed the time of Smith's arrival.
Anastasia said that Dirsey had spent the night of November 11th at the home of her parents and left after a pleasant breakfast on the morning of the 12th.	Anastasia Wallflower of East Birdwatch, Wisconsin, said that she had bought $500 worth of genuine Indian love beads from Dirsey Flowers for resale in her boutique in downtown East Birdwatch.

The hippie-type character, whose name was Dirsey Flowers who had recently dropped out of Southeast Arkansas State Teachers College, was found by police in East Birdwatch, ten miles from Minnetonka.	The president of the bank, Mr. Albert Greenbags, left before the robbery was discovered. He was arrested by authorities at the Mexico City airport at noon on Friday, November 12.
The robbery was discovered at 8:00 am on Friday, November 12. The bank had closed at 5:00 pm the previous day.	Arthur Nodough appeared in Chicago on Monday, November 8, waving a lot of money.
Dirsey Flowers was carrying $500 when police apprehended him and had thrown a package into the river as the police approached.	The vault of the bank had been blasted open by dynamite.
Mr. Smith's father, a gold prospector in Alaska, had died in September.	Nodough always got drunk on Friday nights.
Mr. Greenbag's half-brother, Arthur Nodough, had always been jealous of his brother.	A strange, hippie-type person had been hanging around the bank on Thursday, November 11, watching employees and customers.
Miss Ellington often talked to her brother about being rich.	An Acme employee, Howard Ellington, Margaret's brother, said that a hippie had been hanging around the construction company on Wednesday afternoon.

Murder Mystery

We are going to play a game that will help your discussion skills.

Each of the pieces of paper I'm holding contains one clue that will help you solve a murder mystery. If you put all the facts together, you will be able to solve the mystery.

You, as a group, must find the murderer, the weapon, the time, and the place.

Any time you think you know the answers and the group agrees on the guess you may tell me.

I will only tell you whether all five answers are right or wrong. If part of your answers are incorrect, I will not tell you which answers are wrong.

You may organize yourselves in any way you like.

Remember, all of the clues are valuable.

Time allotment is 20-30 minutes.

When he was discovered dead Mr. Kelley had a bullet hole in his thigh and a knife wound in his back.	The knife found in Ms Smith's yard had Mr. Scott's fingerprints on it.
Mr. Jones shot an intruder in his apartment building at 12 midnight.	Mr. Kelley had destroyed Mr. Jones' business by stealing all his customers.
The elevator operator reported to police that he saw Mr. Kelley at 12:15 am.	The elevator man saw Mr. Kelley's wife go to Mr. Scott's apartment at 11:30 pm.
The bullet taken from Mr. Kelley's thigh matched the gun owned by Mr. Jones.	The elevator operator said that Mr. Kelley's wife frequently left the building with Mr. Scott.
Only one bullet had been fired from Mr. Jones' gun.	Mr. Kelley's body was found in the park.
When the elevator man saw Mr. Kelley, Mr. Kelley was bleeding slightly, but did not seem too badly hurt.	Mr. Kelley's body was found at 1:30 am.
A knife with Mr. Kelley's blood on it was found in Ms Smith's yard.	Mr. Kelley had been dead for one hour when his body was found, according to a medical expert working with the police.

The elevator man saw Mr. Kelley go to Mr. Scott's room at 12:25 am.	When the police tried to locate Mr. Jones after the murder they discovered that he had disappeared.
The elevator man went off duty at 12:30 am.	The elevator man said that Ms Smith was in the lobby of the apartment building when he went off duty.
It was obvious from the condition of Mr. Kelley's body that it had been dragged a long distance.	Ms Smith often followed Mr. Kelley.
Mr. Smith saw Mr. Kelley go to Mr. Jones' apartment building at 11:55 pm.	Mr. Jones had told Mr. Kelley that he was going to kill him.
Mr. Kelley's wife disappeared after the murder.	Ms Smith said that nobody left the apartment building between 12:25 am and 12:45 am.
Police were unable to locate Mr. Scott after the murder.	Mr. Kelley's blood stains were found in Mr. Scott's car.
Solution: After receiving a superficial gunshot wound from Mr. Jones who thought Mr. Kelley was an intruder, Mr. Kelley went to Mr. Scott's apartment where he was knifed by Mr. Scott at 12:30 am.	Mr. Kelley's blood stains were found in the carpet in the hall outside Mr. Jones' apartment.

The Difference

A hundred years from now

It will not matter

What your bank account was,

The sort of house you lived in,

Or the kind of car you drove.

But the world may be

A little different because

You were important

In the life of someone young.

--author unknown

Global Cookies

WHO IS HUNGRY? WHO HAS THE FOOD?

The following activity will help students begin to understand their responsibility as citizens of the world. They will discover how the problem of world hunger is more than a food problem. It involves transportation, weather, commerce, money, culture, religion and politics. The activity involves the student in a learning-by-doing experience through visual and kinesthetic thinking.

THE COOKIE GAME

This compare and contrast activity was adapted from the following resource:

A Guide For Teaching Peacemaking
Madeleine Glynn Tichel and Jo Dee Davis
The Interfaith Center for Peace
30 West Woodruff Avenue
Columbus, Ohio 43210

Prepare for this activity by following these steps.

1. Have in a bag one cookie (candy bar, cracker, or token) for each student who will participate. Do not distribute them.

2. Divide the room into five areas representing the five continents. (Signs will help.)

3. Explain that the students represent the entire population of the world, and they will be assigned to continents according to the actual percentage of the world's population that lives in that continent. Use the chart to determine how many classmates equal the population percentages. (Example: 10% of 30 students = 3.) Discuss the relative numbers of people "living" in each continent.

4. Explain the bag of cookies represents the entire food supply of the world. Tell students there are enough cookies for everybody to have one. Distribute the cookies according to the way food is actually distributed among the five continents. (Example: 30 cookies = 3 for Africa, 1.5 for Asia.)

5. After the distribution, talk about what they see and what they feel. Discuss the implications of this distribution as long as there is productive discussion. You may want to stop the activity and tell the students that the United Nations has met and has decided that the world has to share so that everybody has one cookie. If your group can handle it, you may want to let them play out the activity, even if the cookies are not equally divided and some people get left out. Allow time to talk over what happened and how everyone felt about it.

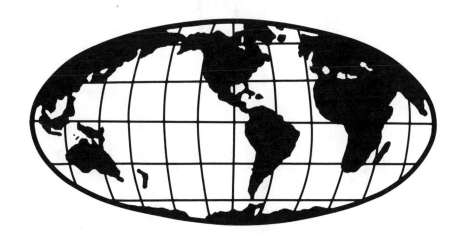

CONTINENT	%POPULATION	%FOOD
Africa	10%	10%
Asia	59%	5%
Europe	17%	25%
Latin America	8%	15%
North America	6%	45%

What would happen If. . . ?
Thumbs Up!

It is surprising how an entire unit of study can be built on just one question. **Thumbs Up!** begins with the question, "*What would happen if human beings did not have thumbs?*" First, students brainstorm the changes that would occur if human beings didn't have thumbs. This can be done in large groups, small groups, or partners.The facilitator encourages students to "*dig deep*" for as many responses as possible.

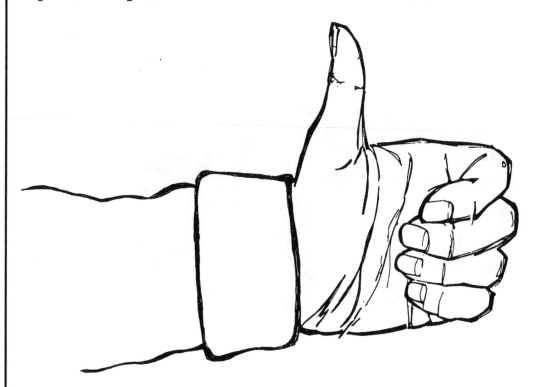

Examples of changes and difficulties:

. . . gloves and mittens

. . . holding a pencil for writing

. . . playing some musical instruments

. . . count by fours instead of fives

. . . buttoning clothes

. . . thumbing a ride

. . . sports/sporting
     equipment

. . . shaking hands

The responses come quickly at first. However, the process becomes more difficult as the brainstorming list grows. It is the role of the facilitator to ask thought-provoking questions that will stimulate more responses. An effective facilitator is patient, stubborn, and persistent. He/she doesn't stop the brainstorming until one more idea has been squeezed from one more student. There is always ONE MORE IDEA!

Just when the students are about to give up and the frustration level is very high (*"Miss Johnson, our brains are dead! We can't think of anything else!"*) the facilitator presents two roles of masking tape. Tear the tape in 3 foot strips and tell the students to tape their thumbs down to the palms of their hands. Students can help each other.

Take the students on a school tour—open doors, lockers, windows. Provide a box of "stuff" (scissors, bowling ball, jar of peanut butter with twist-on lid, eating utensils, and toys) and encourage students to experience a world without thumbs. Ask them to untie/tie shoes, button/unbutton clothes, and sharpen their pencils. Follow with more brainstorming.

It will amaze students and facilitator how many more ideas they are able to add to their list. Learning by doing stimulates thinking.

Thumbs Up! is the beginning of a unit on famous inventors and their inventions. After the taping, have students research inventions that require the human's opposing thumb. Because they have experienced not having thumbs they are keenly aware of its importance in the inventing process.

The culminating activity in the unit involves the students in redesigning something for a human hand without thumbs. What would a pair a scissors that is designed for a human hand without an opposing thumb look like? What would a bowling ball look like? Students will use the high level thinking processes of analysis, synthesis, and evaluation to complete their designs. And it all started with just one question!

Bugs

A Chain Reaction

The following activity was adapted from **Project Wild, Elementary Activity Guide,** *Western Regional Environmental Education Council. Boulder, Colorado, 1986.*

Pesticide pollution is truly a global problem. This simulation is a kinesthetic, learning by doing activity that will help students understand how insects and animals ingest poisonous chemicals.

Cut small pieces of colored construction paper. The pieces should be approximately two inches in diameter. One-third of the pieces should be white and two-thirds multicolored. Scatter the small pieces on the floor of a large open area.

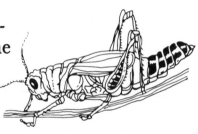

For a class of 25 students, 17 would be chosen to be grasshoppers, 6 field mice, and two eagles. Use different colored arm bands or head bands to distinguish the insects, rodents, and birds.

The grasshopper is given a small paper bag representing his stomach. The grasshoppers are given 30 seconds to pick up as many of the pieces of paper as possible and place them in their bags. The mice and eagles are predators. They sit on the sidelines watching their future prey. After 30 seconds the grasshoppers stop.

The mice are now allowed to hunt the grasshoppers for 15 seconds. Once a mouse taps a grasshopper, the grasshopper is assumed eaten. The grasshopper must give his bag, filled with pieces of paper, to the mouse and sit down.

Now the eagles hunt the mice for 15 seconds. Live mice may still hunt any remaining grasshoppers. If an eagle touches a mouse, the mouse is considered eaten and the eagle gets the food bag. The mouse sits on the sidelines. After 15 seconds the eagles and remaining mice stop.

Ask the students who are "dead" (having been consumed), to identify what insect or animal they are and the animal who ate them. The living animals then open their food bag(s) and count the number of white pieces of paper and the number of multicolored pieces of paper they have. Put the results on an overhead, chart, or chalkboard.

Discuss the meaning of the words **pesticide** and **ingest**. Discuss the chain reaction that begins when farmers use pesticides in order to have a healthy crop to sell. Insects ingest pesticides, mice ingest the insects, and eagles ingest the mice. Therefore, many pests are killed, but other animals die as a result of the pesticide. Farmers never intended mice and eagles to die, but they do because of the chain reaction.

Tell the class that the white dots represented the pesticides and that living and nonliving grasshoppers would all be dead if they had a single white dot in their food bag. If mice had half of their dots white, they would also die. The eagle might not die, but runs the risk of having thin egg shells which would be too weak to hatch its young.

Pizza Wheels!

This is a great activity that can extend across the curriculum and be used all year long. It will help your students expand both their oral and written vocabularies. Your local "pizza palace" can be your business "Partner in Education" by donating pizza wheels—all sizes to your class.

Have students find the middle of the pizza wheel. Have them, using the bottom of a paper cup or a compass, draw a circle around the middle point. Then have them draw 3 or more diameters in black marker, careful not to draw through the circle.

Give students or have students draw circles from colored paper the size of the middle circle. Have them write nouns—all kinds of nouns—one on each circle. Then have them pick one noun and lay it on the circle on the pizza wheel.

Next, have students brainstorm words they relate to the noun on the center circle. They can write them in the "Pies" of the pizza.

Use another noun with a new pizza wheel and repeat the process individually or in groups.

Keep the pizza wheels that have been filled with words in a learning center or special place. During the year when students have a topic to write about, they can place the topic on a circle and place the circle on any of the wheels to help them think of words, phrases, and ideas to write about.

As an alternative, the pizza wheel effect can be drawn on plain paper and duplicated for the students. They can then cut out the wheels and the centers.

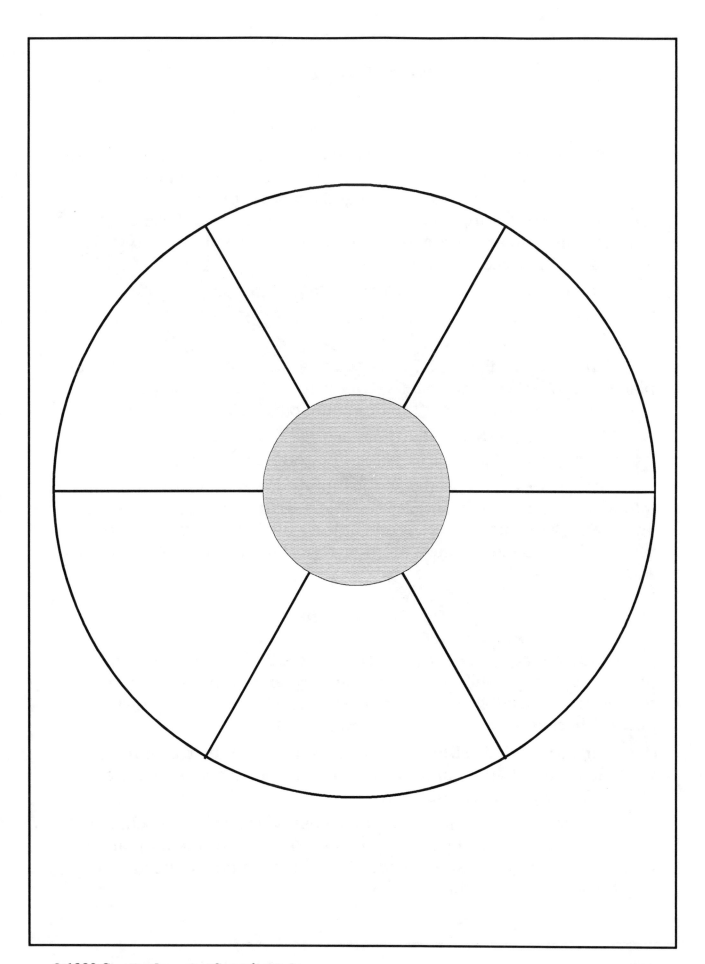

Paper Airplanes

There are many ways to practice the art of brainstorming. It can be done alone, in partners, small groups or large, written or oral, on paper, walls, or transparencies. It can be words, pictures, shapes, or all of the above. A simple and fun way to brainstorm different kinds of questions is to ask students to write an idea or subject at the top of an 8 1/2" x 11" piece of paper.

Then everyone folds their papers into paper airplanes.

The teacher signals, GO! and the entire group flies their airplanes around the room.

The teacher signals, STOP! Students pick up other students' airplanes, unfold them and write a divergent question on the paper about the subject written at the top of the page.

The students then re-fold the airplanes, fly them again, and when they retrieve another airplane, they add a second question.

The process is repeated several times. Each time students unfold airplanes they read several questions written by other students and then try to add a different one of their own. The activity is completed when students write a story or report about the topic and questions on one of the airplanes.

More airplane ideas

Story Starters: Each student writes the beginning of a story on a piece of paper and folds it into an airplane. A "*write, fold, and fly*," pattern is established. After several repetitions of the pattern—*voila!* There is a story written by several people.

Flying Math Problems: Students make up their own math worksheets and fold them into airplanes. Whoever gets the airplane completes those math problems.

Airplane Spelling: Students choose words from a spelling list or dictionary that they know how to spell. They print them on an airplane. Whoever gets that list of words must learn how to spell them and then be tested by the writer of the list.

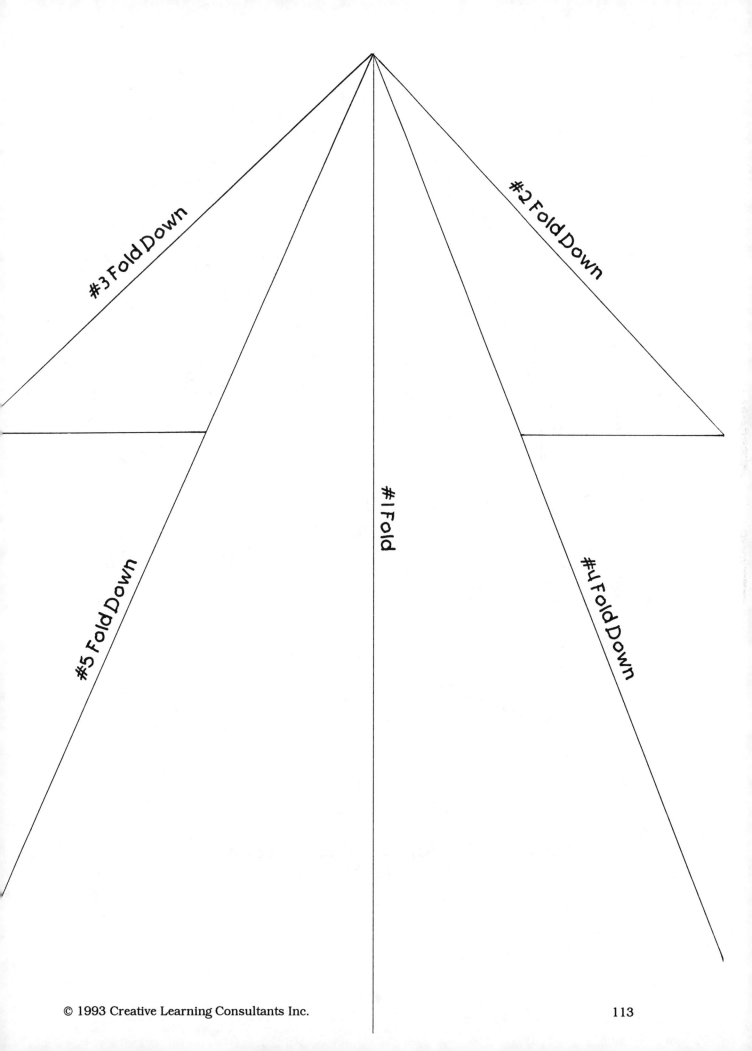

#3 Fold Down

#2 Fold Down

#5 Fold Down

#1 Fold

#4 Fold Down

habitats

What would happen if the earth had another Ice Age?"

What would happen if you had to live in your car?

List all the different kinds of reptile habitats.

Make a list of questions a spotted owl might ask an unemployed logger.

How does the changing of a distant habitat affect you?

What is the difference between houses and homes?

Why do some mammals live in trees?

Would you rather be a bed in a space station or a bed in a submarine? Why?

Compare and contrast a gopher hole with a hotel.

What are all the ways a person can construct a shelter for himself?

114

It's Not Knitting, But...

It's soft. It's colorful. And, if you pay attention to the sales, it's cheap! It's also one of the best teaching tools available. Tie enough 12 foot lengths of yarn in circles so that groups of five students have one circle. Students stand in a circle holding onto the string with both hands, facing the middle of the circle. The teacher/facilitator proceeds with the following directions:

Math — Language Arts — Geography

Using your circle and the people in your group, show MORE THAN inside the circle and LESS THAN outside the circle. Now show LESS THAN inside the circle and MORE THAN outside the circle.

Show more than three, less than five. Show less than two, more than zero. Show a circle that is half full of people. Show an empty circle. Make a perfect SQUARE shape. Everyone hold on!

(Teacher/facilitator continues asking for different shapes: equilateral triangle, isosceles triangle, standing right triangle, pentagon, hexagon, two triangles, three triangles, a five pointed star, etc.)

Each group with yellow yarn make a square.

Each group with blue yarn make a triangle INSIDE one of the other yellow squares.

Note: The yarn can be knotted every centimeter or inch and used for a lesson on area.

Each group lay your circle of yarn on the floor. Form a simple outline of a butterfly with your yarn. Transform your butterfly into a SAD butterfly. Then a POWERFUL butterfly. Then a COMPLICATED butterfly. Then an INSIGNIFICANT butterfly. (As a follow-up students write a story about a butterfly.

Each group lay your circle of yarn on the floor. Form the outline of your state.

Can someone in your group point to the capital city, the county with the highest population, the cities where each group member was born? Is someone in your group standing in another state? What is its name?

Note: The yarn can be used to make states or countries next to each other or one inside another for compare/contrast purposes.

Yarn Puzzle

Once in awhile an activity comes along that facilitates different learning styles, stimulates thinking skills, motivates cooperative learning and is fun. This yarn puzzle is a topological puzzle that can be used as a springboard for a group discussion about three life support skills for the 21st century: (1) increased tolerance for **frustration** (2) practice in breaking **mindsets** (3) learning how to learn through **partnering.**

Give each student a piece of yarn about four feet long. Arrange students in partners. The yarn puzzle is created by tying the ends of each piece of yarn around the wrists of each student, making sure the pieces of yarn are interlocking before the last end is tied.

For example, student **A** ties one end of his blue yarn around his right wrist and the other end around his left wrist. By doing so, he has created a complete circle with his yarn and body.

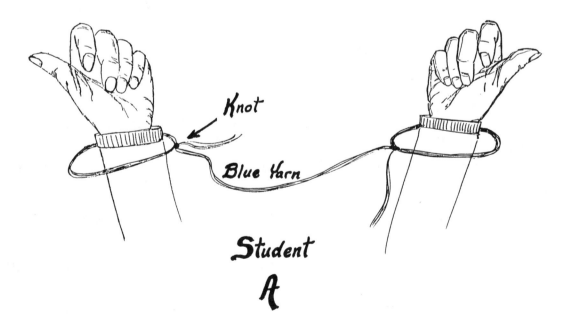

Knot

Blue Yarn

Student

A

Student **B** loops or hooks his yellow yarn through student **A**'s circle of yarn BEFORE he ties his own yellow yarn on to his own

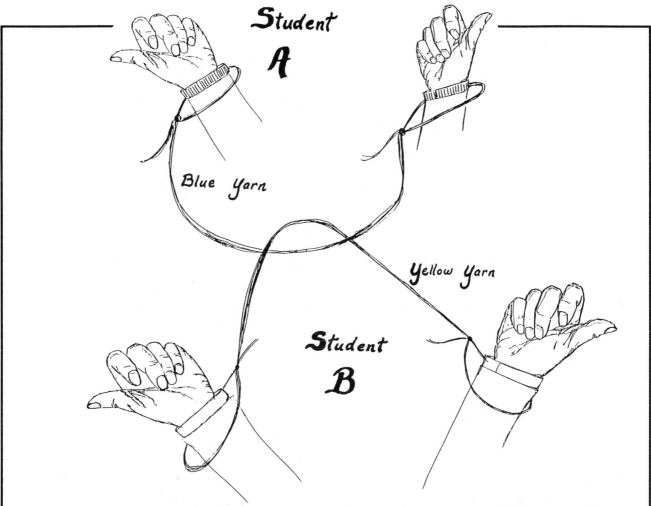

Student
A

Blue Yarn

Yellow Yarn

Student
B

wrists. The result is a yarn puzzle consisting of two interlocking pieces of yarn—one blue/one yellow. The ends of the blue yarn are tied to partner **A's** wrists and the ends of the yellow yarn are tied to partner **B's** wrists.

Students now try to solve the puzzle (unhook the two circles) WITHOUT cutting, breaking, untying the yarn, or slipping it off the wrists.

SOLUTION: Only one person is the solver. The other partner does nothing. In each partnership one student must volunteer to be the solver. For purposes of this explanation student **A** will be the solver.

Partners face each other. Student **B**, with yellow yarn, extends both hands, about a foot apart, straight out in front of him. Student **A** (the solver) positions both hands in front of his own face. He then extends one hand forward between **B's** hands. Student **A** must push the CORRECT hand forward. He must push the hand that allows his blue yarn to hang free below his partners yellow yarn. It isn't always the right hand. It all depends on how the yarn is tied. Student **A**, the solver, can experiment by first pushing his right hand forward, then drawing it back and pushing his left hand forward. Only one of these moves will result in his blue yarn hanging free below his partners'.

The solver's hand that is pushed forward, between **B's** hands, does all the remaining steps. If the solver's forward hand happens to be a RIGHT HAND, he then completes the solution process by following these directions:

Solver (student **A**) uses his right hand to reach down and grasp his own blue circle of yarn which is hanging down from his right wrist. He runs his yarn down the LEFT arm of student **B**, starting at **B's** shoulder and ending at **B's** left wrist. When the solver gets to his partner's LEFT wrist, he sticks his blue yarn through the top of **B's** yellow yarn that is tied in a small circle around **B's** wrist. The solver must be careful to stick his yarn from the back, pulling his blue yarn forward through the small yellow circle. As the solver pulls his yarn through he should be holding a loop of blue yarn in his right hand. The solver then drops the open loop down over the front of **B's** left hand. The solver then lets go of the loop and backs up. Voila!! **A** and **B** should be free from one another. If not, untangle the knots you have made, retie the puzzle and try again. If all else fails, get the scissors!

If the solver's forward hand happens to be a LEFT HAND, he then completes the solution process by following these directions:

Solver (student **A**) uses his left hand to reach down and grasp his own blue circle of yarn which is hanging down from his left wrist. He runs his yarn down the RIGHT arm of student **B,** starting at **B's** shoulder and ending at **B's** right wrist. When the solver gets to his partner's RIGHT wrist, he sticks his blue yarn through the top of **B's** yellow yarn that is tied in a small circle around **B's** wrist. The solver must be careful to stick his yarn from the back, pulling his blue yarn forward through the small yellow circle. As the solver pulls his yarn through he should be holding a loop of blue yarn in this left hand. The solver then drops the open loop down over the front of **B's** right hand. The solver then lets go of the loop and backs up. Voila!! **A** and **B** should be free from one another. If not, untangle the knots you have made, retie the puzzle and try again. If all else fails, get the scissors!

118

If The Shoe Fits . . .

Go to an office supply or teacher supply store and purchase some string tags. (buy the largest size) Write a shoe related question or activity on each one and tie them in a bunch on a old shoe. Voila! You now have an instant moveable learning center. Students can answer the questions as part of their seatwork or homework. Encourage students to bring an interesting shoe from home. Teacher provides the blank tags. Students compose the questions. Voila! You now have 25 instant moveable learning centers!

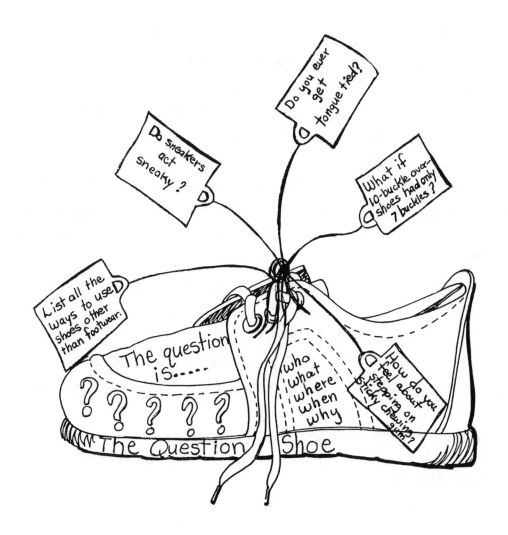

Sample questions for the tags might include:

Do a shoe survey of your family. How many pairs does each member have? How many different colors, styles, conditions (old/new),or values are they? Graph your results.

Miss Johnson wears a button that says, "If the shoe fits, buy it!" Why?

If shoes could talk, what would a pair from America have to say to a pair from Japan?

What does "These boots are made for walking" mean?

Which came first—shoe buttons, shoe hooks, shoe buckles, or shoe laces?

Write a story about a pair of neon colored shoe laces that saved a little girl's life.

Where in the world are shoes NOT found?

Look down at the shoes you have on right now. What kinds of really neat stuff could you add to make them unique?

List all the things a shoe doctor might do.

Draw a picture of an ugly shoe monster that ate Cleveland, Ohio. Ask a friend to write a story using your illustration.

Do you think Americans should ONLY buy shoes manufactured in America? What is your opinion? What is your grandmother's opinion?

Which is more practical—sneakers or boots? Write a debate between the two.

What if it were against the law for adults to wear shoes?

Draw a pair of shoes with at least 25 different details.

What is the history behind penny loafers? Are they only worth a penny?

Describe 3 different shoes. Don't name them. Ask a classmate to read your descriptions. Can they guess the name/style of each shoe you described?

List all the things shoes CAN'T do.

Think of some famous feet. Draw a pair of shoes for them.

List things that shoes might step in or on each day of the week.

What do you think the owner does while wearing this shoe?

Tape a radio/TV interview with the owner or write a story about a day in his/her life.

Where has this shoe been? Draw a cartoon story about his/her adventures.

What are all the things you can do with shoes besides wear them on your feet?

Draw a mindMap with shoes as the focus. (make a BIG mindMap—use butcher paper)

How does it feel to be "walked on" all day? Write a poem or story that describes the shoe's feelings.

If shoes could talk, what would the left one say to the right one? What would they say to socks, toes, sidewalks? Write a dialogue (a play) between the shoes and act it out. The shoes can be like puppets—you could even make them "talk" by cutting the soles loose so the "mouths" will flap.

Write four-word sentences. The four words should begin with
S-H-O-E.

Example: Sing **h**igh **o**peras **e**lsewhere!

Write a story or poem about the time in your life when you were trying to learn to tie your shoes.

How would it feel to be a horseshoe?

How can shoes make money for people?

What does it mean to be a shoe-in?

Describe the life cycle of a shoe.

Describe the life cycle of a shoe store.

Compose a Bill of Rights for shoes.

Who do you think wore this shoe?

Compare/contrast tennis shoes and sneakers.

List all the materials that shoes are made of.

Write a story about cowgirl boots or ski boots.

How far away in miles, blocks, and feet, is the nearest shoe store?

 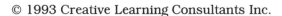

Write a conversation between Michael Jordan's shoes and a basketball.

How could a pair of shoes get you in trouble? How could they get you out of trouble?

Design a pair of shoes that would allow you to walk on water.

Explain what brake shoes are.

Estimate the number of shoes in a shoe store at the mall. The next time you visit that store check your estimation with the manager. How close were you?

Ask you parents, grandparents, and great grandparents, to describe the styles of shoes they wore when they were growing up.

What if 10-buckle overshoes had only 7 buckles?

Compose a song or rap about a pair of shoes.

Compare/contrast the price of shoes. Graph your results. Do you think some shoes cost too much? What is your opinion?

Interview a podiatrist using a list of questions related to shoes and healthy feet.

List all the careers related to manufacturing and selling shoes. Which one would be your choice?

Think of what a pair of sandals looks like. Now draw a pair of muddles.

Draw a family tree for a pair of shoes. Use funny, crazy, outrageous names for each family member.

Search the yellow pages in the phone book for different references related to shoes. Challenge yourself and a friend to find as many as you can. List them in a shoe dictionary.

Oh no! Your favorite pair of shoes just died. Write an obituary or tribute to your shoes.

How many steps do you take each day? Count the number of steps you take in one hour? How big is each step? How many steps in a mile?

DEAR SHOES ...

Letter writing is a wonderful opportunity for students to practice their active questioning skills. Letters usually include many DIFFERENT questions from the writer to the reader. Sometimes it is easier to write DIFFERENT kinds of questions if the writer is sending a letter to someone or something that is DIFFERENT. So . . .

Break that mindset! Take a risk! Don't just write to people. Write to a pair of SHOES!

The following letter and questions can be used as seatwork. (PASSIVE QUESTIONING) Have students pretend they are a specific kind of shoe. Have them answer the letter. The next letter should require students to compose their own questions. (ACTIVE QUESTIONING) The people, subjects, or topics of future letters might include the following: famous people, a candy bar, a landfill, a monkey in a zoo, a jar of peanut butter, the city of Minneapolis, snowflakes, the Bill of Rights, a button on the uniform of a Civil War confederate soldier, the color green, a marshmallow floating in a cup of hot chocolate, a rubber band, a swarm of killer bees, a raindrop going through the water cycle, Lady Macbeth, a store in the mall, a football, a race car, a watermelon seed, a magic monster, a tree in the Amazon Jungle, a bill in congress, Lindbergh's plane (Spirit of St. Louis), a letter in the U.S. mail, one calorie in a cookie, the First Lady's favorite necklace, the number 42, the biggest book in the library, a broken pencil, a decaying tooth, one of Julia Child's mixing spoons, an NFL super bowl ring, a corsage pinned on the mother of the bride's dress, a wheelchair in a nursing home, a hic-up, etc.

DEAR ...

How old are you?

Where did you go on vacation last summer?

What is your favorite song?

Do you like being smelly?
What kind of socks are your best friends?

Would you rather stomp in a puddle or sleep under a bed?

Do you have any high heeled friends? I heard that high heeled shoes are kind of snobby. Is that true?

My favorite color is blue. What is your favorite color?

Is your owner a nice person?

Do you ever honk your shoehorn?

What happens when you go to the shoe hospital?

Do you know any famous shoes?

How do you feel about stepping in sticky chewing gum?

Would you rather walk on asphalt, marshmallows, or broken glass?

Do you ever get tongue tied?

Do you leave tracks when you walk?

Did anyone ever try to steal you?

Are there grandma and grandpa shoes in your family?

If you could give yourself as a present to someone or something, who would it be?

YOUR FRIEND,

The Super Shoe

Have students design a shoe either from the past or for the future. They might elaborate using everyday things like wheels, motors, wings, or floats. Or they may include items from their environment like watches, clothing, radios, or Nintendo! Ways to fasten may be "ordinary" like snaps, zippers, buttons, or velcro.

Or they may invent another type of fastening. As they create their super shoe, have students think about WHY the shoe is made/shaped as it is. When they have finished, create a symbol or logo. Then have them develop a one-minute commercial to give to the class.

"stuff"

stuff (stuf) n. 1.a good fundamental material of which anything is made. 2.things, belongings, fabric. 3.an artistic product of unspecified kind. 4.Informal, a special skill.to do one's stuff. 5. to fill up. 6.to fill or cram into an opening. 7.to pack tightly. 8.TO DO GOOD STUFF---THE ONLY STUFF!